Perfect Earth

LeeAnne Maurhoff

I0553416

Cover Image License obtained from Adobe Stock Images.

I dedicate this book to Jessica, Chase, and simpler times.

CONTENTS

ACKNOWLEDGMENTS

This book came out of a time in my life where everything was uncertain. It is laced with imagery of my beloved hometown and the places I have traveled. It has provided me the opportunity to explore my demons and my creativity. I will forever be grateful for all those who helped bring this story to life.

A special thanks to my parents, Bruce and Vonnie Maurhoff for always encouraging my creative side and goals. Thank you for sitting in the living room and listening to the very early stages of this book that were merely ideas in a notebook from my childhood bedroom. You continuously encouraged me to keep going even when I could not see it going anywhere at all.

Thank you to my sister-in-law, Abbie Maurhoff, for letting me hang out with the best brainstorming mate. Carter Maurhoff thank you for listening to me talk through this book. I know you did not have choice since you were an infant. You surely did protest many terrible ideas.

Thank you to my siblings Chase Maurhoff and Jessica Tomlinson for making my childhood full of adventure and letting me believe in fantasies for way longer than most kids got the chance to. I am so lucky to have such supportive loving siblings in my life.

Thank you to my brother-in-law, Sean Tomlinson for taking the time to fully edit my book and for sharing my love of reading. I will always treasure the feedback received from the most avid reader I know.

Thank you to Shri Hari R. R. for putting time towards my passion. Thank you for your continuous support.

Finally thank you to all those who contributed to this book going into publication: Franklin Edwards, Sarah Atique, Shalini Rana, Gargie Nagarkar, Katherine Wagner, and Gabby Franzone.

Chapter 1

Twelve

~ *Ella* ~

My name is Ella James Hollington. I have always hated my middle name with a passion. Perhaps it's because I do not know where it comes from. I do wonder if my parents always secretly wanted a boy. I have asked them why James? They both reply that they just like the name, which means my mother picked it. My father's name is Bob, which is even worse than James. He is hard working, which is the only attribute I can tell you about him. He is always working.

As a child, I thought maybe he was a spy, because when I would ask him what he does, he would say, "work is work." Unfortunately, he is not a spy or anything interesting. He is a computer programmer. This is a considerably basic description, but that is all I have gotten out of him. Eventually, I stopped asking. He makes a lot of money, but you would not think so, looking at my little house. It is a single-story, flat house, shaped like a shoe box, poking out of the side of the hill. I always burn candles to combat the smell of the cigarettes, permanently stuck into the walls long before I came into this world. The ceiling is leaking black in spots, as if one day it will just crack open and fall in half.

It does not sound like much, but it is my home.

My mother looks like a rich lady. She has had way too much Botox, which shows in her sunken, hollow head. I have never seen her without a perfect face of makeup. To be fair, in my 18 years of life, I have not seen much of her in general. She runs a fashion line and is always travelling. She and my father have multiple houses throughout the world. This house on the hill is the only one I have ever seen. I used to think they were ashamed of me, but now I know that they just forget I exist.

When my mom travels, so does my dad. He can work from anywhere, so I regularly receive pictures of gorgeous places. They used to randomly show up with gifts from all over the world. Chopsticks from Thailand, a stein from Germany, a bottle of expensive stinky perfume from Paris, and many more beautiful trinkets are on display around my room. If I was in a movie, I might come off as ungrateful or a spoiled brat. I wish that were the case. I am not spoiled. While my parents have a lot of money, I do not. I try to be happy for them, but then I look out my window and see nothing but a hay field stretching out to meet the mountain. Appalachia Virginia. I never thought I could love and despise a place simultaneously like I do my hometown.

I would say who raised me, but in truth there have been so many people in and out that the list would take up half a book. When my parents would come home, they would fire my nanny, hire a new one, and off they would go again. They fired some for reasonable causes. For example, Reese. She used to make me pretend I was a cat and would only let me eat cat food. One day my parents walked in and there I was with a foam cat tail around my waist, eating a cat treat. She got fired and I was extremely relieved.

They also fired my favorite babysitters. Like Mindy. She was a teenager, which meant I automatically worshiped her. One time I told

Mindy that I fear the dark. I explained how everything becomes terrifying when I close my eyes. The next day she brought me lavender puree and told me that no matter where I go in my dreams, it will always bring me back home. My parents came home from their trip to Paris and Mindy did not help them with their multiple bags. She did not help them because she was listening to me tell her some story that I made up as I went. They did not fire her in front of me, but I never saw Mindy again. I cried for weeks and tried my hardest to share my stories with any of my new caretakers. There was Sarah, Emily, Gertrude, Bethal, and the list goes on. Then, my twelfth birthday arrived, and everything changed.

I was so excited to see my parents, even though I knew they would leave. Twelve is a big year and I could not sleep fantasizing about what my fabulous gift would be. Maybe they would even stay a while. Maybe my gift would be to go with them on their next trip.

When they arrived, they naturally took care of my most recent nanny. She got in her car sadly and drove away. I was barely fazed, anticipating the gift, wrapped in silky white paper, with a deep navy-blue bow. Bob took out his camera and videoed me ripping through the beautiful paper. They both smiled as I lifted the lid to the box. My excitement was jolted as soon as I saw my coming-of-age gift. It was not my first pair of heels, or a makeup set. It was just slick metal heavily set in foam. All their talk about me becoming a woman and reaching a new phase of life was celebrated with this hunk of violence. They were celebrating my 12 years of life by giving me a gun. Tears started to sting in the corners of my eyes.

"Look, Ella, we know we are gone a lot and we really just want to make sure you are safe." Bob said. His brown, puppy dog eyes angered me even more.

"Well maybe you shouldn't constantly leave me. Maybe you should actually be a parent, rather than give your 12-year-old a stupid gun!" I yelled.

Then I ran.

I ran through the tall cattail weeds in the hot sun with tears streaming down my face. I went to my favorite place, to wait for my favorite person: my next-door neighbor, Amanda.

We used to run down this same old field behind my house and make up stories in the woods. Every day we were in a different kingdom, world, or universe, talking with aliens. We found this tent, made from branches, and that was our spot. When we started to grow up, Amanda would talk about boys she had a crush on or girls she did not like, and I would listen. I would sit patiently, hoping to get back to the magical things that we created that were truly ours. I guess I missed the memo that your imagination stops as you age.

That day, as I picked ticks off my legs, I laid in the tent, waiting for her to come. I was a few hours early for our normal meeting time. I dozed in and out between dreaming and reality. At some point, I fell fully asleep. Owls whooped, waking me up to the chill of night casting its blanket over me and the woods. She never came. I sobbed and kicked the branches of the tent until a few broke. Once they cracked, my sobs quieted, and my lips quivered. You see, Amanda is the only friend I ever really had. I never stepped foot into those woods again.

I slowly waded through the field with the grass halfway up my legs. My body and mind became overcast with numbness each step I took. By the time I reached the house on the hill, it was pitch black. My parents were gone but left two envelopes with wads of 100-dollar bills. The front of the envelope said *"happy birthday Ella"* in my mom's curly, airy, handwriting. It's like they knew they were leaving for a while this time.

Once again, I was left alone. They left without asking me about my life or what I was interested in. I picked up the gun and looked at the smooth shiny metal.

"It's just me and you buddy. You can protect me like I protect my middle name, James. It's our little secret," I whispered. I got up and went to my bedroom. In my closet there is a little door that opens to an empty metal box. That became James' home.

Twelve was quite a big year for me. I was left with two wads of cash, no nanny, no friend, and no parents. It left me with only one other person besides myself and a deep sadness I still cannot completely shake. I did keep believing in magic and other worlds. I owe it all to the woman who watches me sleep every night.

Chapter 2

Nightmares and Whispers

~Ella~

Every night when I lay down to sleep, since I can remember, the woman who watches me creeps out from the cracked closet door and stands by my bed. As a kid, it terrified me. I used to think if I make one wrong movement, I will lose a hand or my head.

On my twelfth birthday, with the darkness painted across the sky, I waited for her to show. She did as she always has every day since I can remember. My plan was to speak to her and become her friend, but as usual, I was not able to speak or move while she was present. I just wanted to look at her face and see who she was. I wanted to ask her why she spent her nights looking over me. I could not. My entire body was stilled except my brain.

Her shadow loomed over me. Every move I tried to make, resulted in a sensation of a million tiny needles prickling under my skin. I started to sweat and felt my heartbeat quicken. I could not move one muscle. So as usual, I closed my eyes in my panicked sweaty state, and she guided me through my nightmare. I was falling and falling through black space reaching for help. Blinding lights came over me and I knew I needed to escape. I couldn't. I just kept running into metal walls with swirly art full of screaming faces. She grabbed my hand and led me to a door. As it started to open, I woke up.

This dream on my 12th birthday was nothing new. I have a couple of repeat nightmares that she continues to guide me through. When I first wake up, they feel so real. It's almost as if they are not actually nightmares. They almost feel like an old memory. Like they are part of me and my experiences. It's as if we are exploring my past. Except the events have not happened. Not yet anyhow. They all end the same way most of the time. When they do have different endings, she gets annoyed and the phrase *"you are not listening"* repeats in my head as I wake up.

One recurring dream that I vividly remember and still have, is the most terrifying. I find myself standing in front of a jury, while a girl in navy blue, with sparkling blue eyes, claims I should be murdered; then she winks at me. A dart comes towards me, and everything blurs out. I then wake up in the dream to a horrid smell and feel a weight pressing down on me. The weight, I realize, is from a pile of dead bodies, and the woman who watches me tells me to climb out. She tells me I can make it. I push and push and as soon as the sun shines through the hands, arms, and legs that are decaying around me, I wake up.

The smell of leather and glue always fills my nostrils as I come back to reality. Then the lavender puree on my nightstand rescues my nose and I am back in my bedroom. When I wake up, I am always disappointed she is not here. I wish she could always be with me. Even when I have been more alone than I thought possible, she always gives me a purpose when I close my eyes.

There is one reoccurring nightmare she has never been able to save me from, which I have about once a month. In it, I am all alone, searching and searching for someone who I cannot find. Suddenly, a blinding white light shines all around me and shoots through my body. Throughout the white light I see flashes of tiger eyes, a man yelling, and smoke filling the air. I wake up covered in sweat and the watching woman is nowhere to be found. These are the worst nights. When I am not haunted by her, I am haunted by myself.

I have always been strange, or at least that is what people say. Living in a small town, you always know what people think about you. It is like everyone has so much space to yell in, that they never learned how to whisper.

This became apparent to me on my first trip to the local Piggly Wiggly a month after my twelfth birthday. I drove my dad's hunter green beat up Volkswagen. I had driven it through the field behind the house but never with other cars on the road. So, I was on edge and a little shaky when I walked into the store smelling of old meat and rotten fruit. The whispers started. "The poor dear, I hope she hasn't gotten into drugs like Mindy's granddaughter" "They start younger and younger these days" "The little thing is going to get dreads if she doesn't learn how to brush her hair" "She is such an interesting little thing. Never says a word". This was just the start of the whispers I have continued to hear.

My parents have been bad at sending money throughout the years, which has resulted in my style not existing. I can tell that the girls at school snicker when I walk by in my flared jeans and faded t-shirts. Middle school was hard, but a lot of girls did not have style then and we were all transitioning. High school has been unbearable.

In movies, the skinny blond with blue eyes always wins. You see, I have these features, but I have somehow ruined them. My hair is straw-like, not shiny. This is probably due to years of using the cheapest shampoo I could find at Piggly Wiggly. Makeup is something I have never worn. It is an unnecessary expense. I am thin, but my clothes have been a size too small for most of school. This results in bulges where you do not want bulges. I walk around looking like a lumpy scare crow. It is not too bad, as people eventually stopped looking at me at all.

I did not receive another couple of wads of cash until my fifteenth birthday. It came in a huge box, with paintings from Paris. I was down to splitting boxes of spaghetti in eighths when it arrived. When my last nanny got the boot three years earlier, I had to learn how to cook. Spaghetti was my diet.

I was going to burn the paintings at first, but the fat strokes, bringing the canvas to life, were too beautiful. Why would I ruin these pieces of art? They are not the ones who left. They are hung up in the kitchen now.

Thankfully, my parents have been sending wads of cash in six-month increments since.

At least during my last year of high school, I have looked somewhat normal. More money equals better clothes. However, I am not normal, according to the corny movies I watch on TV. With a house to myself, I have never thrown one party, stolen alcohol out of my parent's liquor cabinet with a group of giggling girls or had a boy over. I do steal alcohol out of my parent's liquor cabinet for myself, but I do not think drinking alone counts.

Overall, I was not the most sociable child, which has made me grow into a hermit of a young adult. I am about to be 18 and be a 'grown up', but I also know, in my bones, that there must be more than this. Yes, I spend my time reading fantasy fiction and being alone. Maybe I fantasize about being the underdog lame girl who finds the secret door to another world and becomes the hero. Maybe I am just becoming too invested in the books I try to live in. Maybe I want more because what I have is just me and that is not enough. Maybe the woman watching me is just a sign that I am clinically insane. Or maybe, just maybe, there is another world that I am being called to and magic is real. Regardless, I know I am meant for more. Maybe I can find a purpose when I am awake too.

Chapter 3

Tiger Eyes
~ *Ella* ~

I walk to the kitchen. My eyes roll at the paintings of Paris. It is habit now; I barely catch my eyes doing it. It would absolutely piss mother off. She would go on some long rant about how I should not disrespect such cultural pieces. Although they are just paintings of the Eiffel tower, which they sell prints of at every home decorating website.

I grab a bowl from the black cupboard that has paint chipping away at the edge. All our bowls are different. Mother says it gives the kitchen character. I imagine they go off to a mansion somewhere, where all their dishes match. I take my bowl that is now full of left-over ramen to the handmade wooden table that has four chairs and sit at the farthest one. They bought it for me the last time they came home, since our other table broke. I told them I put my elbows on it and it came crashing down on my leg to explain how it broke and to also explain the long scar that now scales down my calf. In truth, I drank a little too much, and stood on the table, performing a skit for all my imaginary fans. The table came crashing down, and my calf landed on a large chef's knife. I had used it to cut the limes accompanying my tequila. The lime juice zinged my leg, as the knife sliced its way into my flesh. I liked the sensation. I think about it every now and then when I trace the clean crisp scar.

I stare at the liquor cabinet, contemplating grabbing the aged whiskey. Tonight, is my eighteenth birthday.

I spent the day posing next to a tree for the school yearbook. Everyone else's parents brought them. Mothers doted over their daughter's make up, while fathers stood together, having awkward conversations that they pretended to enjoy. I stood off to the side, reading until it was my turn. I know that when I see the pictures, I will laugh at the air-brushed versions of myself. I will probably not even buy any.

Tomorrow, Mother and Father will be getting back from their most recent trip. Mother called last night and said they would like to have a talk about college with me. I wonder if they know I have already applied and been accepted.

Some parts of college sound exciting. Like I get to start over. I will be able to make real friends. The brick buildings, girls with oversized t-shirts (which is now trending apparently), ice-cold coffee, boys with defined muscular arms, soft smiles, and the smell of new books, all come into focus. I will not have to wonder if my parents will come home or feel disappointed. I will have a purpose.

Except, I am not sure if I will. I do not know what to major in. I really like math, but I do not want to study or teach it. I like reading, but am horrible at writing, as far as grammar and all the rules go. Also, I have always been bad at making friends. After Amanda, I really tried. For the few that noticed me at school, it went well. We would hit it off in class, they would come over, and we would have a great time. Then, the next day at school, they would pretend not to know me. It was as if the house is cursed or something. Other than the gas station in the middle of town, there are not many other places to go. Driving forty minutes to a nearby city without a driver's license, just to grab food with some girl I barely know, sounds like too much effort to me.

There has always been one person who has seemed to notice me: Jack.

During that three-year period where money was tight, I would skip lunch at school a lot. Not only because the money. Part of it was not having anywhere to sit. I would always go out the back cafeteria door and read leaning my back against the brick wall. That is where I first met Jack. He was wearing an old jean jacket that was so worn out that his elbows would poke through when he bent his arms. I had heard girls giggle about him in the locker room. How mysterious and quiet he was. I always thought they were being so ridiculous, but when I first saw him, I also wanted to giggle. Which is a teenage mannerism I have always rolled my eyes at. When I sat down next to him for the first time, I sat as far away from him as I could. He glanced up as I ungracefully fell onto the hard cement. His golden-brown eyes made me freeze. He smirked and went back to reading his book.

Over time we started moving closer and closer, towards the middle of the brick wall. We talked a little, but mostly read side by side. He would sometimes bring lunch and would share it with me. I would do the same. These small interactions got me through high school. Or most of it. He never came back for senior year. Rumor is, he just up and left in the middle of the night. I think I get why. He always had bruises and cigarette burns up and down his arms. Or, at least, he did the few times the sun was too overbearing for his jean jacket to withstand.

I was heartbroken that he did not even leave me a note or stop in to say goodbye. However, I do not hold it against him. It probably got even worse in the summer when he didn't have school to buffer the blows. In the end, he is yet another person that has left.

I clank my empty bowl into the sink. I usually rinse right away, but I always leave at least something for Mother to clean, as small payback for the years of abandonment. I walk down the dingy orange hallway with black sneaking in through the top. The old lady who lived here before was a smoker. Father told me one time. He looked like he wanted to tell me more, but just left it at that. Typical Bob.

I crawl into bed and feel excitement creep into my chest. I know it is stupid, but there is always a part of me that hopes they will stay this time.

I am so caught up in thinking about my parents and college, that the woman who watches me is far from my mind. I start to dose off, then I feel her gaze. It is different tonight, stronger. I shut my eyes, trying to control my breath, as usual. Beads of sweat race down my forehead. The nightmarish bright light flashes. I wish this horrible dream, where she does not save me, would end. I just want to see darkness when I close my eyes. My ears start to buzz, as if a million bees are hovering around my head. I can feel every dust particle floating in the air and falling on my body, one on top of another. Am I awake or asleep? The noise, the dense air pressing down on me, and her extremely strong gaze are too much. The light brightens and brightens. I feel as if my eyes are going to liquify and leak out of my head.

BANG!

Everything stops. I sit up and she is gone. All is quiet and the room is frozen. The dust particles are suspended in the still air. My eyes are pulled towards my window. I do not remember leaving the blinds up. I never do. Then I see a woman's shape in the darkness as she lifts her head. The tiger eyes that I have seen over and over in my dreams are staring right at me. Their enigmatic glow makes it impossible to look away or move. I cannot believe it. I always thought I would turn into stone or melt but here I am just looking at this tigress woman.

"Are you ready Ella?", the woman says, displaying pointy canine teeth. With the window separating us, the loudness and clarity in her calming voice surprises me. It is as if we are the only two people left on the earth. Without hesitating, I slide my window up and hop onto the soft damp grass, feeling the strands in between my toes. *This is just another dream*', I tell myself. Deep down, I know she is real and that what I have been waiting for is here. My life has been leading up to this moment.

"My name is Lindsey. I used to live in the house you live in now", the tigress woman says and holds out her hand. I intertwine my fingers with hers. They are warm compared to the chilly night air. I can feel our pulses sync together as we begin to walk. *Lindsey? Use to live* in my house? How can that be? Lindsey was an old lady that smoked like a chimney and died before my parents bought it', my mind is racing with questions.

"That's your earth's version, not mine", Lindsey voice echoes, interrupting my running thoughts.

'Your earth? Implying there are other earths? Where is she taking me? This must be a dream. Should I try running? Would she impale me with her sharp canine teeth?' My thoughts start to unravel, sending my brain into a panic. I watch my feet, one in front of the other, and then they stop. Am I even controlling my body?

Looking up I see we are at the edge of the woods that I have avoided for the past six years. Lindsey starts stepping through the trees and I follow. Her movements are those of a cat stepping carefully and hardly making a sound, as if she knows where each branch lay. I used to know where each branch lay. I look around and my trail is overgrown with leaves, sticks, and other animal tracks. My presence here is gone. Each step I take results in a loud crack that echoes through the still night air. I am so clumsy, almost falling every other step, reminding the woods and myself that I do not belong here anymore. This thought sickens me, as we use to be connected.

The sticks stab the bottoms of my non-calloused feet. The moonlight weaves in and out of the trees, sending a shiver down my spine. Goosebumps spring up on my legs. Of course, it is a full moon. 'Where is she taking me?' Then I see it. I see the tent made from fallen branches. My eyes get watery as I think of Amanda. She should be here too. She should have believed with me all these years. I spot the broken branches near the entrance of the tent. I am not welcome here. I broke the fortress and stormed out never to return. Lindsey motions for me to step inside. Cautiously, I duck down and sit criss-cross applesauce, like I did as a child.

Slowly the earth starts to fall away from beneath me. I try to scream out, but not one sound escapes. I reach for a wall, or something to grab onto, but only black space slips through my fingers. Faster and faster it goes, the wind sending my hair straight up. My ramen dinner flops its way up my throat. My head feels as if there is a large spoon spinning around the ingredients of my brain.

Suddenly, the motion stops and all I see are white blurred lights. The piercing green tiger eyes are over me as everything fades to complete black.

Chapter 4

My Guardian Devil
JACK

I have always been dark and brooding. That happens when life gives you a bad hand. You get drained of your naivety and lightness at an early age. I have bounced from foster home to foster home. Sometimes I would get moved because of their behavior. Sometimes I would get moved because of mine.

I have always tried to behave. To be good. Then darkness will seep over the sky and the black crow will perch herself on my windowsill. My guardian angel or devil. I have still not decided after what I believe to be 18 years. I have lost track of time.

My black beauties name is Sharon. She has led me through all the hard unbearable moments in my life. She has shaped my mind to always keep fighting. Fighting to tear them all down. I have just been waiting for 'the moment'. The moment where I smear all the lines drawn in the sand. These lines that are decided by people who are so far removed from reality. The politicians, rich CEOs, and wealthy who have everything they have because they have profited off people like me.

You see, my dad was an activist. He fought for our people, tried to make things right. My mom died in the hospital giving birth to me. They could have saved her and probably would've if we had the money. If we looked different. No one talks about that though; the truth makes people uncomfortable. I didn't fully lose her then though. I still had my dad, and he did what he could. He worked multiple jobs and kept speaking at rallies and fighting. Until I was three.

He was shot.

It is my first memory.

I don't tell people that. I tell them I lost both my parents when I was three in a car crash. Having your father shot in front of you makes people either wildly uncomfortable, pity you, or they lap it up. They fantasize in your tragedy. They get excited by your pain. It is a story that they can share at the salon, church, the grocery store perhaps all three. They talk about how horrible it is while playing detective. Making up the reasons why it happened. Not because they care, but because it is exciting to have *new* news.

That is the worst reaction; the lapping it up. Unfortunately, it is the most common reaction in my small town. Tragedy's make great stories and headlines except when they are your own.

Sharon helped me through losing my parents. She helped me to see how everything is so unfair and how it won't be fair until you burn it to the ground and rebuild. My dad thought it was through uniting with each other. Look where that got him. I still remember the pool of blood in our kitchen.

As a kid, I was terrified of birds. I thought Sharon was coming to pluck my eyes out in my sleep. My body would freeze, my breath tense, and the air would still. It's like everything stopped, frozen.

Everything was frozen except my heart going double time. My chest would tighten. All my teeth hurt and felt soft as if my mouth was filled with soft mints. The white and red stripped ones given out at Christmas. My brain would twirl and swirl around like a pot of soup on the stove. Despite all this, I just wanted to be able to see her. I could feel her form into a woman. I could feel the air move around to her skinny, delicate, hard figure. I could feel her staring over me. I wished to turn and talk to her.

That is how I ended up here. I wished and she granted it.

I cannot pinpoint how much time I have been stuck in this metal box. That is why I like to journal. This book of leather with milk pages is my anchor through the pain. My dreams here are the same. It's all filled with fire, smoke, and those blue eyes.

Ella Hollington's blue eyes. You see, at school we used to read during lunch together. Except I was never actually reading. I was always glancing sideways at her. She is beautiful, strong, and lonely, like me. Not lonely in a sad way. Lonely in a dark, empty way. Even though her smile is bright, her skin is fair, and her eyes sparkle like blue water in the sun; she is hallow and anger is churning beneath the surface. When I was around her, I could feel the anger and hate. I loved it circulating in the air between us. I have heard you are not supposed to be attracted to people with hatred in their heart, but I dream about her.

The problem with Ella is I have never been sure of where her hatred lies. Mine lies against the world. Mine is molten hot and is about to boil over any minute. I don't think Ella is aware of hers and I get nervous thinking about who will get in her way. I guess none of this matters now. I am here alone.

I am in training in a place called the 'In Between'. I have no idea where it is, or how I got here. I do know why I am here. I am being built into a weapon. That's not what the videos I watch say or what the doctors who slice my bones and make my teeth clatter in pain say. It is what Sharon says. It is what she has been training me for. My moment.

When I first slammed into this place like a meteor through space my head felt heavy, and my eyes felt bleached. It has been the worst punch I have received so far. Trust me, I have received a lot. Sharon slipped into my room. Not the crow I have seen before, but the woman I had felt transform next to my bed for years.

She is beautiful. She has black eyes, jet black helmet hair, and the ivory almost translucent skin with her green veins mapped out beneath the surface. Her nose, elbows, and knees are all sharp. Her lips are thin, but in a mischievous way. Her voice is high pitched but demands the room. Her movements are jagged and smooth at the same time like a digitalized bubbling brook buffering. I cannot remember if she slipped into my room when I was in bed back home or when I was laying on this paper-thin cot here. I drank a little whiskey before bed, so my brain was sloshing around. I slightly remember walking outside, then I slammed into this room. I do not know if it was the arrival to this cold metal room without windows or the vomiting, but I sobered up pretty fast.

She said a lot in those blurry moments of me leaving my bed at home and ending up here. I do not remember it all, but I tend to remember certain pieces when I write this story over and over. I like reliving my past because as they shave away and whittle at my body, it's the part of myself I can keep.

I have written over 200 entries. Sometimes I write a couple times a day. Sometimes I am in a hospital bed for weeks at a time going in and out of consciousness. My brain has never fully settled since that bottle of whiskey. I am pumped with meds. If I am sober, I write because my aching body and brain are too much to just sit in. I have no idea how long I have been here or how long I will stay. I just know whatever happens, my guardian devil will be with me whispering in my ear.

"Jack you are embarking on a journey. The toughest one you have taken so far. Just remember we must burn it to the ground before we build it back up. The end is never the end in the universe. We will whittle it all down to ash and out of that we will rise. We, my love, will rise."– Sharon whispers a nightly terrifying lullaby in my ear.

Chapter 5

The In Between
~ *Ella* ~

I slowly open my eyes to a bright rectangle light that is slightly buzzing. Turning my head straight forward, a large horizontal rectangle window, with three empty seats, is directly in front of me. White walls with vinyl padding stretch out on all four sides of the rectangle. I am in a white padded room. My body pulsates as my heart takes over. My head is aching, and my eyes burn from the brightness of everything. I blink and pain surges from my temple to my eye.

Am I in an insane asylum? Is it one of those social experiments? If you see the tigress woman and follow her, she turns you in and takes out the cool contacts. Was she even real? Have I been imagining her for 18 years? Did I murder someone and not remember?

Then she appears behind the long glass window. Her green eyes lock with mine. The swirling thoughts and air stops, and my pulsating body slows, as I breathe in and out. A hand interrupts our locked line of vision. I see two other people have entered the room behind the glass. I strain my eyes as they come into focus. A man with a large nose and handlebar mustache is standing to the left of Lindsey. He seems to be explaining something, moving his hands in a flowing motion towards me. The woman on Lindsey's right is completely still. Her beady black eyes are looking off into the distance. Her jet-black hair hugs her face, as if she is wearing a helmet. Strangely, she resembles a vulture, with her long skinny nose, hands, and entire figure.

Where the hell am I? I need to demand they let me go! I move, but my body goes nowhere. Looking down, I see a thick grey bands across my chest. I try to move forward and realize my waist, thighs, and calves are also constrained. I wriggle as hard as I can before a jolt of pain shoots down from my neck. Hot blood trickles down onto my bare chest. *What have I gotten myself into?* Tears, blood, and hair start flying everywhere. It is as if I am watching someone else moving. "LET ME GO!", I scream and wail over and over. This must be a dream. It is all a dream.

Then, with the same clarity, volume, and calmness as outside the window of my bedroom, Lindsey's voice is in my ear, *"it's okay Ella. Calm down. I am here and will always protect you."* She pauses, letting me once again find my breath. I take a deep breath in trying to place the lavender besides my bed. Instead, the room smells of stale lemon air like a dentist's office. *"You have been chosen to save the universe. You are here to fully live out your purpose. This is what you have been waiting for. We are going to leave and give you privacy. Please shower, get dressed, and try to not cause yourself more pain. Do not take too long, your partner is waiting. We will explain everything in detail. Most of all, know that this is where you are meant to be."* This echoes in my ear, as if she were speaking through a loudspeaker, but her lips did not move once. I can still feel the aftermath of the vibrations of her voice shudder through my skull. *Can she communicate with me through her mind?* I think about all the times she has spoken with me. *On the way here did she speak out loud then?* It was so dark. I look at her behind the window. She is explaining something to the guy with the handlebar mustache as he exits their observation deck. The vulture lady does not look at me once, following him quickly. Lindsey pauses and smiles a smile that says, 'I promise you are okay.' There is a twinge of sadness in it. Oddly enough, I do feel as if I am okay.

Exiting, she pushes a button, the straps loosen, and I step down onto the cold white tile floor carefully. My legs are like half-cooked noodles as I tumble onto the ground. I catch myself with my hands and slowly rise.

I am completely naked.

Hot embarrassment rises to my cheeks. They all saw me naked, and I somehow have not noticed this very embarrassing detail until now. Anger fills me as my thoughts ride the ripple of this emotion. *How could they just strip me down? And what the hell is in my neck? 'Your partner is waiting for you.' Who is my partner and for what?* I spot the enclosed shower behind me and a little table with navy blue scrubs besides it. This weird institution is not the magical fantasy world I had imagined as a kid.

It seems like days before I hear a soft knock on the door to my 'room'. It has probably only been an hour. I had tried to escape, but the door was locked and there is no window. I also did not think to grab my phone before I followed Lindsey into the woods. Even if I had, who knows if it would work here. I do not even know where 'here' is. So many questions have floated through my head. *Where is my bed? Who is my partner? Can I also communicate telepathically? How am I going to save the universe?*

I also have been practicing what I would say to her. *'I demand you let me go. How dare you cut my neck and strip me bare.'* However, as soon as she opens the door, my tongue fills up my mouth like a dry sponge. I quietly follow her out of the room and try to memorize the winding hallway, filled with abstract paintings and metal walls. I am looking for some sort of escape route, but cannot even manage to locate another door, window, or anything but metal.

We come to a halt outside a beautiful oak wooden door. I am surprised, as I did not see this door as we approached. It just popped up out of nowhere. This all feels so familiar. She motions for me to open it and I do. So slowly.

I am immediately met by the smell of cinnamon and sight of warm orange colors. The furniture is all oak and smooth. The most surprising aspect of the room is the man facing the large projector screen that takes up most of the farthest wall. His brown, almost black, hair is messily piled on his head. He has broad shoulders and defined muscular arms. He turns around looking just as surprised as I feel. Then I realize who this man is. I cannot believe it! It is Jack from school. The skinny, lanky boy, with his elbows poking out through his jacket, is all grown up. I feel my cheeks turn pink and a giggle tries to wiggle its way up my throat. Thankfully, I catch it and shove it back down before it escapes.

I think of that brick wall and how sometimes our knees would touch. That same warmness and electricity that pulsed through our awkward bodies is now circulating between us in the air. I wonder if he feels it too. We stand in this warm room of a possible insane asylum, looking at each other in silent comfort. His eyes have dark circles around them, but his eyes themselves light up as our gaze continues. Or maybe I have imagined that too.

"You hungry?", he asks hoarsely, motioning to the burgers that sit on the round table between us. He warily takes a seat and dips a fry in a tub of ketchup. I sit quietly, too into my thoughts to respond. I have missed our meals together. I start to study his body. On each of his muscular arms there is a giant scar stretching from the middle of his forearm to the middle of his bicep. Moving my eyes up towards his face, I am stopped by the perfectly spaced out and circular scars on his neck. They look like the cigarette burns he had on his arms in school, but more precise. His face has lost its roundness. It is chiseled, but not in a strong features' way. It is chiseled from exhaustion and pain; you can just tell. He looks so much older.

Lindsey enters the room right as my gaze lands on his eyes, which seem to have been watching me throughout my scan. I am immediately ashamed for staring. I just cannot believe he is here.

"We will play a movie for you both. Please pay attention. While Jack has already seen this film, we believe it is beneficial for you to watch it together. After all, you will be embarking on this journey together, as a team. We will come back for questions at the end. Enjoy your food", Lindsey says while only looking at me. She exits the room, and the projector screen lights up with four planes, each containing an earth.

A man in a hunter green and off white horizontally stripped sweater pops up on the screen. He is white with dark hair and his green eyes match the sweater. Apparently, his name is Mike, he explains, and he is going to take us on a journey. I almost snort and glance at Jack. He is not amused.

It reminds me of our outdated health class videos from school. The video shows four quadrants each containing an Earth. It zooms in on each Earth with horrible clunky sound effects accompanying glitchy movements.

"Earth #1 is referred to as 'Global earth' due to the global dependency the countries have on each other to survive . Earth #2 is referred to as 'Perfect Earth', due to its economic and environmental wealth. Earth #3 is referred to as 'Equal Earth'. Earth #4 is referred as Power Earth." Mike says very enthusiastically. The movie does not go into a detailed description of the last two Earths. This makes me slightly thankful, since I am still trying to figure out what the hell is going on.

"All four Earths exist simultaneously. This is possible through the sixth dimension. We currently live in a four-dimensional world: height, length, width, and time. The fifth dimension goes into a reality mirroring your own. For example, if there was an earth identical to us, with the same exact people on it, it serves as an alternate reality. The sixth dimension goes into multiple alternate realities and allows varying factors. For example, you do not necessarily exist on the three other Earths." Mike explains as if he is just telling us about simple male anatomy.

"So where are you right now?" Mike continues. "You are currently in the 'In Between'. You are in between the four alternate realities of the universe. Why might you ask? You are going to serve as 'sliders' and transition to one of the other earths to help set an injustice right. That is our purpose. Helping set an injustice right brings positive frequencies to all dimensions resulting in more positive energy pulsing through the universe. When we emit positive energy, this results in positive reactions. Your positive deeds will emit throughout the universe. Who knows? You might prevent a murder, an earthquake, or a sickness!" Mike smiles as he bobs his head to silly music and the words 'The End' appear in a cheesy font. The screen then goes to black.

Jack and I sit in silence. I have scarfed down the entire burger and fries, while he nonchalantly swirls the same fry in a tub of ketchup. I look up, finding his golden-brown eyes welling with tears. Without thinking, I grab his hand and hear myself saying, "It will be okay Jack."

He shoots up abruptly and starts pacing annoyed, "No it is not okay Ella! It is not. I have been seeing this lady every night as long as I can remember. She has taken me through these horrific events in my sleep. I was in my soft bed, and she shows up with her beady eyes. "Susan, my name is Susan, and I have an adventure for you", she said.

"She led me to my childhood treehouse and BAM. I was brought here. I do not even know how long I have been here Ella. My last memory on Earth was sitting next to you, leaning against a brick wall. It seems so long ago, I do not even remember the book I was holding, or the food we were sharing. I was worried I made you up. I have been through so many medical procedures and have taken so many pills, everything is foggy. I have seen this movie over five times, and I still do not know if it is true or if this is just a way to prolong my torture. Then the beautiful Ella Hollington walks in. We have been microchipped and now we are going to 'slide' into another dimension of the universe. So, no, it is not okay, but to be honest, seeing you makes it better." He sits back down in his chair just as quickly as he got up. He does not look surprised or embarrassed. Even with his abrupt venting, Jack is in complete control. He has always been this way. Controlled and calm.

'He thinks I am beautiful' circles around in my mind, but I say, "So you have been trapped here this whole time? I was told you ran away. I thought you just left without saying goodbye."

"Ella I am so sorry. How long has it been?" Jack replies, staring at the floor. His foot is tapping violently waiting my response.

"It has just been a year, Jack. And I promise, you did not miss much. Senior year has been just as uneventful and mulling as the other years of high school." I lightly laugh to try to make this come off as a joke.

"That is not as long as I had expected. They say I only have one more big surgery left. That is not where the pain will end for me. I am used to it, though, but I will say you did get the lucky end on this one, Ella." He leans forward and puts his head in his hands and starts to rock back and forth. I honestly have no idea what he is referencing, but I immediately feel guilty. I want to ask him a million questions. It is not the right time.

"We can make it through this together, whatever this is. I promise." As I say this, I really do hope it is true.

"Yeah, it will be fine. So, what books have I missed?" He looks up and smirks at me. A giggle manages to roll out of my mouth before I can shove it back down this time.

Chapter 6

A Humble Childhood
[Lindsey]

Holding my warm coffee so close the heat runs up over my face burning my eyes, I head back towards Ella and Jack. I look through the window of the warm room, watching them be human together. Ella says something that makes Jack laugh. The way their eyes light up when they look at each other makes me long for their world. I almost tap into her head, but stop myself, knowing I will be invading her thoughts regularly soon enough.

I start thinking about all the sliders that have been sent before them. How Susan and I just finished shadowing another mission to prepare for our first one as guides. Only one of the sliders made it back. The questions arise in my head for the billionth time. Should we remove these kids from their lives and possible happiness? Are they too young to know what they are agreeing to? These questions are irrelevant.

I do not have a choice.

Steve says they are considered adults and their own world sends them off to fight each other within their planet. He says why not get them to fight for the whole universe, rather than a country in one of the four dimensions. I imagine him producing these words under his ridiculous mustache. I am not sure if I agree, but I know at the end of the day there is nothing I can do.

I feel, in a way, that Ella is my child. I have always been there for her. Protecting her is why I am here. Watching her and Jack's innocence takes my mind to a simpler time.

I remember growing up in obedience school. My room was like the one Ella and Jack woke up in. They isolated us, preparing us for a life as a Humble. Still, I was a child with a curious and playful mind. I used to sneak out of my window running into the jungle behind the continuation facility in Fernweh. There was this pool of water where I saw my reflection. Mirrors were not allowed in the facility, so seeing myself fascinated me. My frizzy hair shone in the moonlight and my brown eyes rode along the ripples in the water. That was my spot. I would always make it back in time for roll call, feeling more alive than if I had gotten a wink of sleep. I visited my spot regularly up until I was eight; that was when they took me.

Many couples and families would show up behind the glass window in my room. Sometimes the facilitator would allow me to hear their words and sometimes they would not. They all looked the same, white ivory skin, dark hair, and bright blue eyes. A part of me understood that they were on the other side of the glass because of the way they looked. I had a very surface level understanding of how the world worked back then.

The day Master Sam and Master Ally came in felt different. Most potential Masters smiled or at least said hello. Not them. While Master Ally's eyes were blue, they were not bright or lively. It seemed as if a shadow had been permanently cast across them. Master Sam followed behind her, looking tired. His eyes were sunken into his head.

He reminded me of this creature I saw by my spot one night. It was grey and had dark circles around its eyes. The creature was kind and held my finger with its tiny hand. I could see the same kindness in Master Sam.

Master Ally was speaking to the facilitator and stopped mid-sentence when she looked at me. Then her mouth curled up on one side.

"Would you like to say hello?", the facilitators voice echoed through my room.

"No, but she is the one I want", Ally said.

"Great, we are glad to hear that. It is tradition to pick a 'familiar' form, we recommend an herbivore. I have a list of regularly chosen 'familiars'", the facilitator said.

"A tiger", Ally replied abruptly.

"We do not really recommend tigers here at this facility. That might result in a danger for our patient or yourself, as it has not been done before. It could be dangerous, even after the procedure is completed." The facilitator started to wring his hands nervously.

"A tiger. I will pay all extra fees. As far as danger, I would love to see the silly little creature try against me. Besides, I like a challenge." Ally's sneer reached me to my core. I wanted to run into the jungle and have my finger held by the black-eyed creature with tiny hands.

"Very well. The procedure might take longer than the normal waiting period of two years. We will promise a three-year waiting period. Does that suit you?" The facilitator opened the door to lead

Master Sam and Master Ally out of the room behind the glass. Master Ally's eyes did not leave mine until the door shut with a loud bang.

The chills that went down my back, thinking about her eyes locked with mine, were nothing compared to the painful procedures I underwent for the next three years. I would sometimes wake up with four paws. Other times I would wake up with two hands. I was changing back and forth. One thing was consistent. The pain. The aching. It was guttural and struck my core. I was just a mass of scars, bruises, and shaved bones. I barely ate and barely got to go to my spot. When I did sneak out, my body was so sore. Climbing down the side of the building, I could feel every twinge and ache jolt from my head down to my toes. When I would get to my spot, I would look at my bruises and puncture wounds and cry.

I did not understand back then why a human being would put another through such torture. Now I do. People value being comfortable and feeling like they are right over empathy and kindness. That is why Masters take human children and turn them into animals. They do not want to feel bad for the way they treat us. They do not want to be reminded that we are human too. They want to comfortably keep us below them at all costs.

Remembering those three years of laboratory appointments, tears, and pain makes my bones shudder inside me.

I find my eyes on the verge of tears as Ella and Jack come back into focus. They will have to embark on the same journey. Shorter and better technology, but I have no doubt in my mind there will still be pain. Especially Jack since he is assigned a familiar. Judging from the cigarette burns and bruises he had when he arrived, we figured he would be okay. He has, surprisingly, done very well. Susan told me over and over he has been tough since he lost his parents.

They will both fit into their roles well enough. I just cannot shake this eerie feeling about this mission. The thought of reconnecting with the world I have been running from turns my stomach inside out. Steve interrupts my thoughts by appearing beside me, stroking his mustache.

"Ready to take them to the next phase of training?", Steve asks in his archaic professor voice. I resist rolling my eyes.

"Yes sir", I reply, and we enter the warm room. Ella and Jack get extremely silent, as if they just remembered the reality of their situation.

Chapter 7

The Mission
~ *Ella* ~

"I hope you enjoyed your meal. My name is Steve. Lindsey, Susan, and I are a team with an especially important purpose. We lead sliders like yourselves to other dimensions to right injustices. When negativity is turned positive, this radiates positivity through all dimensions, as you were told in the movie. That is our goal is to push more positive energy into the Universe.

You are from Earth #1, Global Earth. Your mission will be to slide to Earth #2, known as Perfect Earth. It was deemed as Perfect Earth by the agency we are part of, due to its lush environment and lucrative economy. However, like every Earth, it has flaws.

It has one of the harshest class systems of the four dimensions. This class system is split into two groups, Masters and Humbles. Masters make 8% of the 6 million population. They are the wealthy class, averaging an income similar to $1.2 billion on your earth a year. Humbles are the poor class, averaging $2 a day. Humbles have various roles. Humbles can be raised in the family continuation unit, work in factories, restaurants, cleaning companies, and many other production focused roles. Humbles in the family continuation unit do not make any money. They are isolated as a baby and raised to serve. At the age of 5, a Master can select them and can choose a familiar for the Humble. Many do, as it has been a tradition for decades. The transition period is 2 to 3 years, placing a Humble with a master at the age of 7 or 8. For example, Lindsey's master chose a cat as her familiar. She can shape shift into a cat. Before the age of 5, she was a normal child."

I look at Lindsey when he says this with my jaw dropped. She does not seem to notice and shows no emotion as he points her out. I shut my mouth immediately.

He continues, "Due to a Humbles ability to morph into an animal, Masters start viewing them as such. Working Humbles are not assigned familiars, but due to their status, they are not viewed anywhere close to an equal either. Overall, Humbles are viewed and treated as slaves. They are misused, abused, and are at the expense of Masters, regardless of which sector they are in. Many of them live among trash, as $2 a day is not enough for a proper life. That is why you are here." He presses his lips together, causing the bottom of his mustache to disappear into his mouth. He looks as if he is trying to convey an emotion, but it seems he might have heart burn.

Lindsey picks up the silence, "Your mission will be to help a factory of 200 Humbles escape. We will train you in your roles, Perfect Earth's rules, and our expectations. It is extremely important you pay attention during training. A wrong move on Perfect Earth could result in significant loss or death. The society is not as understanding as your world. There is a region of free folk in the south. You will be leading the factory's Humbles there, without being followed or discovered. Once you complete this mission, we will slide you back here. No earlier and no later.

You are embarking on a journey to bring a positive impact to the Universe. It is important that you keep this big picture in mind to make the correct sacrifices. You will be placed in a house next to Elizabeth, the factory owner." Lindsey's voice catches and she pauses for a moment clearing her throat. She clenches her jaw and continues, "It is your goal to contact her and offer to help with the factory. She is a key piece in infiltrating the factory." Lindsey clears her throat again but seems unable to find the words.

Susan steps up besides Lindsey, which surprises me, as I did not even see her flit in. Her screechy, shrill, throaty voice pierces the air after hearing Lindsey's smooth voice ride along the waves of space. "Ella, you will play the role of Master. This decision was made based on your fair skin and bright blue eyes. You will have to go under slight facial reconstruction to strengthen your features. Of course, we will also need to fix your yellow hair. You will not feel any pain." She says all this while not making eye contact with me.

"Jack, you will be Ella's Humble. As you know, we have chosen your familiar to be a deer, since it is a common one. You will undergo your last dose of transformation surgery. This surgery will take two weeks. It will be the most difficult session you will have. We can reverse all changes once you complete your mission if that is your wish. You will not feel pain." She says the last line looking at Jack with her beady eyes on the verge of tears. The way she looks at him is the way I have always wanted my mother to look at me. It is full of concern and the wildness of true dedication. As if to say she never wants any pain for him, but knows it is not in her control. She is Jack's Lindsey. She is his protector.

The words start to roll through my mind. My throat feels thick, and the taste of metal arises, as if I have been sucking on an old nail. I will be a Master and Jack will be my Humble. That is what he meant by getting the better end of this deal.

I am still in complete shock that a society would turn humans into animals. I do not understand. What is even crazier is that Jack will be able to turn into a deer or maybe already can.

Steve looks at us both and says, "We will give you the night to think it over. Lindsey and Susan will be your guides throughout this journey. They will be able to track your location through the microchips implanted earlier. As you might have already noticed, they are also able to communicate with you telepathically. If you decline this mission, we will remove the microchips and send you on your way, under the condition that this is never spoken of. If you accept, you are embarking on a journey to help those in need and the universe will forever be thankful."

They all exit the room one by one, leaving Jack and I alone once again.

No pressure. *The universe will forever be thankful.'* What does that even mean? The silence between Jack and I increase, and it is too much. My mind is reeling for the 50th time today.

"What are you going to do?", I ask.

"I am terrified. Either way I am tiptoeing through life. Which is why I already accepted. I was given the choice when I got here a year ago." Jack looks aloof, his eyebrows furrowing together. I still have not wrapped my mind around the fact he has been down here, his body being sliced and prodded, for a year.

"Either way I am going into the unknown. I either start college and get to meet more people who think I am too weird, or I am traveling through time and space to help increase positive frequencies in the universe. Whatever that means. I never thought these would be my two options. This is insane. Honestly, I am so alone. My parents will not even notice I am gone. I would rather go somewhere unknown with you than be by myself in the world that I know." I blush immediately. That all came out wrong. He is going to think I like him.

"Ella, I am alone too. My parents died when I was three. I do not even remember their faces. Ever since then, I have been in foster homes. I've been with the Carlias's for the past 5 years. They treat me okay when they are sober, but when Mr. Carlias drinks…." He pauses and clamps down, causing his jaw to protrude out of his chiseled head. "If I stay, I will just keep working at his mill and tip-toeing for the rest of my life. That is why I agreed. I thought I was going to be in this alone. I have been anticipating meeting my Master, hoping that whoever they chose would be better than back home. Trust me, I would rather tip toe around you than him." He looks directly at me. My heart starts beating a little faster and I feel myself blush once again.

"Even if you are part animal? What is up with that by the way?" I ask. He starts busting out laughing in a way I have never seen him laugh before. I cannot help but to join in. This whole situation is so absurd and that laugh decides it. I am traveling to an alternate universe with Jack.

Chapter 8

Beautiful Distraction
JACK

Sharon crept into my room the night before Ella's arrival. "Jack, you will be getting a partner for your journey. One you might know and be fond of. A distraction. But please stay focused and do not share our mission. This person will be your Master and will be yet another person holding you down. Another person who is selfish and, in the end, only cares about themselves. Can you handle that? Can you promise to not get distracted?" Sharon screeched.

"Who is it?", I asked. Every person who has thrown a punch, kicked me out, and used me flashed through my head.

"Ella J. Hollington." Sharon paused awaiting a response. I did not answer. "You can't let her know our plan. You can't let her get to you. She doesn't care about you. In the end she will always choose herself. Never you. You understand that right?" Another pause. I tried to speak but my mouth was dried out and felt furry. I rolled my velvet carpet of a tongue around in my mouth trying to remember how to make words. Eventually, I nodded my head. Sharon did not stay by my bed and irritably left the room.

That was a couple days ago. I had practiced my reaction to Ella entering the room for an hour the next morning as if we were meeting for a first date. I was not practicing out of nervousness, but to win her over. I need her on my side while keeping her at bay at the same time.

I know I sound cold, but I am not the boy she sat next to in high school with the bruises down his arms and cracked ribs. I have been altered. Not just in body, but in mind. As always, I am a tool in the grand scheme of things. This time, I am a tool that will give purpose to the greater good. I am a tool that will win.

Miss Ella thinks she is here to save slaves. I'm sure that makes her feel so good. I can picture the self-righteous savior complex written all over her face. We are going to go in and save the poor. That's what the agency tells us they want, but I know the truth. Everything governments do to 'help' those in need, is to get good pr while researching ways to keep people in their appropriate place. While Ella comes in on her white horse gassing her head with an inflated ideal of herself, I will get the info I need to tear the Earths down one alternate reality at a time.

I will say seeing those eyes today made me a little bit wobbly. When I see her, I am with her, and I feel human again. I do not feel like the animal they are making me into or the atomic bomb I have been groomed to be my whole life. I feel like me. She has also jolted my memory. I have started remembering how I ended up in this metal torture hell in the first place.

Sharon showed up in my room like every night. The energy she brought was different. It is like her and I were connected on a deeper molecular level. We were sharing the wave lengths in the air. Her breath was my breath. She led me to the window, and I opened it. I followed her to the treehouse I had built in the woods behind the Carlias's house. She motioned for me to climb, and I did. When I sat down, I started to fall. At first, I thought a board was loose. Then I kept falling surrounded by black space and then I was thrown down on a floor. When I woke up, I was strapped down and Sharon was there. She was just watching me.

Ella is helping my memory. She has turned out to be more useful than I originally thought. I cannot meditate on this thought too long. When I walk away from Ella, I try to turn these thoughts off. I hone in on my mission with Sharon. I am back to surgeries and studying in the dark.

I am worried, how will I separate myself from my memories when we get there? I need to make sure I tell her what she wants to hear. Keep it simple. Sometimes I wish how I come across to Ella would be true. I want to feel things.

At this point, I do not know if I was ever able to feel anything. Maybe I have been lying to Ella the whole time. I wanted to be the boy she crushed on. The one boy who made her feel seen, because it made me feel normal. I am not normal, nor have I ever been. Nor are my three counter parts. I am excited to meet another part of myself in Perfect Earth. The knowledge I will gain in the end.

Steve, Lindsey, and Ella think Jack from Perfect Earth is dead. He is the one who found Susan. Who found me. We are all connected. We are the rebellion. The true rebellion, not the 200 people Ella thinks we will save. The whole movement. The funny thing is, even he does not know Sharon and I's full plan. I am even keeping secrets from myself.

"The most successful people, remove themselves from their own mind. They give up their emotions, their soul, and themselves to be what the people want. People who can master this can rule the world and have done so. You my darling will rule it all" – Sharon's nightly lullaby.

Chapter 9

Purpose
~ *Ella* ~

The next four weeks are a blur of information, pain, and sacred time spent with Jack. I feel as if I am watching it all take place. Then I have another reconstruction appointment and I am slammed back into my body by the pain.

My face aches all over. I try to lift my head and the heaviness brings me back down. Never in my life have I felt so stuck and miserable. They took away my cool scar on my leg. The one from the drunken knife incident. I wanted to ask the doctor to put it back. That is part of who I am. I plan to tell him, but the room fades out every time I try to talk to him. His pointy nose is all I know of his face, as that is the last thing I see as the white room fades to black.

The appointments stop after two weeks. Our days are filled with more movies briefing us on the rules. That is when Jack and I are once again reunited over bowls of soup.

Walking into the room, I cannot wait to see him. Should I hug him, or would that be weird? What should I say? What will he say? These blushing schoolgirl thoughts racing through my head are halted when I see him sitting in the oak room.

He is there first, as usual, but this time is different. He is hunched over, in a wide chair which I soon realize is a wheelchair. His hair is tousled, but not in the messy way when we first arrived. It is matted with sweat. I take a seat next to him.

"Hey Jack", I say. He does not move, seemingly fixed on a spot on the ground. He does not just look tired, he looks broken. He is leaning to one side, as if holding his torso up would be too much of a task. Then his brown honey eyes latch with mine. He does not say anything. He does not have to. I try to smile but the pain shoots up my bruised face. I grab his bowl of soup. I start spooning it into his mouth, bit by bit. He cries silent tears the whole time but does not motion for me to stop.

At the end of our soup meal, we are each handed a mirror. My face is how I have always wanted it to look. I am still slightly bruised, but beautiful. My features are strong, and I look as if everything that would come out of my mouth is a fact. My cheek bones protrude out under my eyes and my strong jawline accents the bottom of my head. I love my reconstructed face and my smooth chestnut hair. I even love the navy-colored suite that I will be required to wear. It brings out my blue eyes. I immediately feel guilty.

Today is the last day Jack will likely look in a mirror. His face is hollow. Not from surgery, but from all the food he has barely eaten. He looks very much the same.

The biggest difference is his eyes and clothes. His eyes have a spark in them I have never seen before. I do not know what the pain has ignited within him. His clothes are bright yellow, tight, and have smudges of dirt on them. They hug every curve of his body, and he looks like a bright, slightly-bruised banana. He scowls in the mirror from his chair at the horrid color. I grab his hand and give it a few pumps. When I was walking around bulging out of my tight clothes, he did the same for me.

Steve walks in for our next training session. He is wearing a tweed jacket and carrying a pointer. He truly looks like a professor. His steps are loud, demanding the oak room even though Jack and I were already quieted by our new looks.

"Do you know why Humbles wear bright clothes?" Steve asks looking back and forth between us. We both nod our heads no. "So, they can easily be spotted. Please take a seat." We are both already seated. We side glance at each other, unsure of his weird overly confident energy. He is taking this training very seriously.

"Today we are going over a lot of material so pay attention. To start off, you can only travel to dimensions you do not exist in. This is why you are able to slide into Perfect Earth. Ella your parents were born into two different classes. Your mother a Humble and your father a Master." This makes me smile an ironic smile as I think about how she acts like she is in control of the world at home. They are different classes of people in both worlds, it seems just opposite. They always have been, and, in my world, it is what makes them work. In Perfect Earth it is what keeps them apart.

Steve glances at me then continues. "Jack your parents are both master's on Perfect Earth, but unable to have children. They own a Humble, but never assigned it a familiar. It is indicated that they treat this Humble as their own." Jack also smirks. I assume he amused how in both dimensions he and his parents are not able to have one another. It is funny, the games the universe plays.

"Now that is the why, but how will you do this? How will you be successful in an alternat reality? This is the most important and incredulous information you learn in your first week of recovery." Steve turns around and pulls a string beside the projected light. A large paper falls down labeled 'The Rules'.

THE RULES

1. Humbles may not look at a master directly in the eye. **

2. Humbles may not use the same facilities as a Master. **

3. Humbles may not steal from a Master. Immediate punishment is loss of a limb.

4. Humbles may not murder. Immediate punishment is death.

5. Humbles may not lie. Immediate punishment is loss of vocalization.

6. Humbles may not disobey. **

7. Humbles may not leave a Masters side. **

8. Humbles may not walk through Masters' neighborhoods after dark. **

9. Humbles may not touch a Master. **

10. Humbles may not own property. Immediate punishment is jail.

***The Master decides the punishment in front of the agency board.*

"Please read these rules carefully and learn them by heart. Going forward you will be required to recite them every morning. Understood?" Steve looks at us intently until we both nod nervously.

He continues. "The 'Agency Board' is Perfect Earth's form of government and justice system. The board consists of elite Masters. Their total system of justice relies on the decisions of people at the top. Punishment details are up to Masters to decide. If you lie or talk back a Humble could lose a vocal cord, tongue, lips, or all three. If a Master disobeys these rules, they will be put on trial and will receive a similar punishment if found guilty." I raise my hand. Steve nods in my direction.

"So, people who do not even understand the lives of the Humbles determine all the rules for them? Also, how often are Masters charged as guilty when all their friends are the ones calling the shots?" I ask appalled and angry.

"The court is mainly used for Masters to perform punishments on the Humbles in front of an audience. As far as people at the top making decisions for all the rest, isn't that kind of how the universe works? Is it all that different on your Earth Miss Ella?" Steve says his eyebrows raised. I want to defend Global Earth and give examples of how much better our justice systems are. I want to tell him we do a better job.

In my 18 years of life, I have not watched the news. I do not know how my world works at all. All I know is my house on the hill and my own loneliness. I shut my mouth and stay quiet the rest of the training.

Lindsey administers our fourth week of training in the In Between. I am glad to see her walk into the room. However, this week is by far the hardest. While our bruises and soreness fades, the practicing of our roles is raw.

Jack is always looking at the ground and avoiding my eyes. It just makes me long for them even more. Any time he looks at me or speaks to me out of turn in our public simulations, I must press the virtual buzzer. The virtual buzzer is basically a shock collar for Humbles, except it is programmed and invisible. Rather than shock him, I leave it on the vibration setting. When I do this, he knows to turn into his familiar. If he does not, he is officially disobeying, and that is when I am required to issue punishment. Of course, if we both play our parts correctly, punishment will not be necessary.

If someone on the street sees him disobey me and reports this to the authorities, we can be taken to trial, and I will be publicly forced to perform a punishment. If I do not, I will be punished myself, along with him. Telling him to transform into his familiar is a punishment in of itself, as it not only reminds him of his place, but is also painful for him, especially in the beginning. His scars are still raw.

Lindsey warns us that it is particularly important to not keep him in his familiar too often and to avoid this transformation as much as possible. Basically, it is easier for both of us to follow the rules from the start. Jack also must sleep and eat on the floor. It is not necessarily a rule, but it is the social norm.

The first simulation when Jack turns into a deer upon Lindsey's orders shocked me. His body completely changes. A smooth brown coat of fur ripples up his body. His chest caves in and his hands turn to hoofs. His eyes stay the same golden brown. Jack does not seem upset; he is still as stoic as always.

I do not understand how contorting someone into something they are not would ever bring anyone pleasure. The people on this Earth must be crazy.

This process is now a normal part of our day. It still makes my heart ache watching him writhe into the beautiful creature. But now I can do it without even blinking an eye. I am proud that I have mastered hiding my emotion towards him. However, I mastered this long before coming to the In Between.

The one comfort we both have is we are not alone. This is something we both have longed for our whole lives, company. Not only do we have each other, we have our protectors. Susan and Lindsey will be with us throughout the mission. They can communicate with us telepathically. They can get in our heads and help us through whatever will come our way. While usually this would creep me out, it has been the one comfort I have taken throughout this training.

. . . .

Jack and I sit, enjoying ice cream in the oak room in silence. We both know that later in the middle of the night we will slide into Perfect Earth. After all the soup, salads, and healthy vegetables, ice cream has never tasted so sweet. I try to eat it as slowly as possible, resulting in a melted puddle of sweet cream left in my bowl.

"Jack, I do not want to hurt you. You know that, right? I will not enjoy ordering you around in any way." Saying these words out loud makes me feel so guilty. Part of me knows this is a lie. I have never felt more powerful and confident than I have in the last week in simulation with Jack. I wonder if he feels lower and more insecure than he ever has.

"Ella, we are here for a mission. We will both play our parts, leave, and go our separate ways. That's it." He sounds like he is forcing the words through gritted teeth. Does he resent me already?

"It might not be that simple," I fling back at him. Tears start to rise and my nose tingles. Then without warning they flow. Drop by drop, ruining my bowl of melted ice cream.

"Hey, come on Ella, don't cry. It will be okay. I am sorry, I am only tired. Remember, whatever this is, we will make it out alive." He embraces me in his warm arms, and I let myself cry on his dirty bright yellow shirt. He smells like pine trees. I breath in trying to lock this moment in my brain knowing it might be a while before we embrace like this again.

Chapter 10

Fernweh, Perfect Earth
~ *Ella* ~

The transition is much like that to the In Between. Except this time Jack and I are not crawling into our childhood hiding spots.

Lindsey and Susan lead us through the matrix of metal hallways and abstract art. We are standing in front of a painting of chaotic swirling colors. Within the colors are peoples screaming faces, just like the ones from my dream. Lindsey takes my hand and opens the door. I half expect to wake up, but I do not. There are four portals with glass doors. They look like showers. Lindsey leads us over to the one labeled 'Perfect Earth'.

"You will enter the portal and sit on the ground just as you each did when you slide here. We will enter the coordinates and you will arrive in Fernweh, Perfect Earth. Most who slide to other alternate realities are called by other parts of themselves. We are tinkering with the way of the universe. That is why being diligent, focused, and fast is important to this mission. Understood?" Lindsey says.

We both nod and she pulls me into a big hug. Susan also hugs Jack. We both step back from our guides, take a deep breath and grab hands as we step into the portal. We sit criss-cross applesauce like children with our knees slightly touching. We can hear beeps as Lindsey enters in the coordinates. The ground starts to sink beneath us. I give Jack a comforting smile that turns into an empty scream.

We fall through black space until BAM.

A very extravagant house comes into focus. My first glance, however, is cut short by me looking at the ground and suppressing vomit. Jack is completely fine, as usual.

When I finally feel stable enough to stand up, Jack looks like his eyes are about to pop out of his head. Then I take the first real look at our not so humble abode.

White marble tile flows up to meet a cherry wood staircase spiraling up. The top of the stairs has a huge statue that flows up almost meeting the extremely high ceiling. The statue consists of gold geometric shapes. To the left there is a cherry wood kitchen table big enough for ten people. The walls echo the grey within the white marble tile. Following the grey walls through the dining room I am led to a surprisingly small kitchen. Which I remember is for the Humble to be in, not a Master.

I leave to go up the stairs and notice the huge living room to the right. It has all mauve couches and chairs, cherry wood nightstands, and a marble fireplace that goes up to meet the high ceiling. I climb the stairs to find three beautiful bedrooms with king size beds and fluffy pillows. Why on earth would a person have this big of a house just for themselves and a roommate? I pick the room with the biggest closet that is already lined with navy blue clothes my size. I scream in excitement as I jump on the bed. Even the bathroom is absolutely gorgeous. There is a beautiful, gold framed mirror, showing my beautiful, strong-featured face, lit up with a smile.

My gleeful exploration is cut short when I rush down the staircase to tell Jack about my fabulous room. Jack stands at a door next to the bottom of the staircase that I did not even notice. I am about to ask why he is staring into a closet, then I realize what this closet is. It is his room. It has a small cot. There is another door in the back containing a tiny bathroom that belongs in an old rusty RV.

"You know if it is just us here, no one will know if you sleep in this little room or not. It can be our little secret. There are three bedrooms up–", Jack walks into the tiny room and slams the door in my face. I do not see him until the morning when he is making my breakfast.

I walk downstairs from the best sleep of my life to the smell of eggs and bacon. "Jack, I had no idea you could cook!" I exclaim as I sit down at the table.

"I slipped a welcome note under the next-door neighbor's door, saying we would like to introduce ourselves. I said we would come over around 2PM. I signed your name on the note" Jack says without looking up.

"Thank you, Jack. Will Elizabeth be able to read it with your chicken scratch handwriting?", I say smirking at him attempting to flirt. He does not look up.

I swallow my first bit of eggs down hard. "What do you say we go explore? We have the time!" I say.

"Yes, let's go explore the infamous Perfect Earth" Jack says sarcastically, while shooting a side smirk over his shoulder. This makes me feel better about whatever animosity is between us. Maybe he just had a bad night's sleep.

Fernweh is beautiful.

It is a white, pristine city, with splashes of color and navy. Masters all have similar variations of navy suits, dresses, and casual clothes. They are completely clean, plain, and all look the same, with dark brown hair and bright blue eyes (just like me).

I have wanted to fit in my whole life, but this is a little too much. I can barely tell my reflection apart from those around me. My love of my new face and chestnut hair diminishes with every step. The Humbles are all following their Masters around and have the same tight brightly colored clothing Jack wears. Attention is immediately brought to every imperfection they have as the bright clothing accents every bulge and bump. The Humbles all nod and smile as they pass the other Masters. Their kindness surprises me.

The Masters do not move a muscle. They are also wearing leather gloves and seem to be wary of touching anything. I see Humbles open every door to shops, cars, and restaurants for their Master. One Master drops their hat on the ground. Their Humble rushes over to pick up and carries it trailing behind the man who does not even seem to notice.

I take note of all of this and remind myself to not open one door.

Suddenly, a nearby Master sends a shock through their Humble. The kind, colorful person transforms into a small, dirty dog.

It looks painful, as they moan throughout the transition. I look at Jack and, for the first time, he looks absolutely terrified. I notice other Masters disapproving stares at my glance toward Jack. I realize I forgot his shocking device at our new home. I need to do something.

"Do not ever do that to me or you will get worse", I snap at Jack. He quickly glances down at the ground, and we continue our stroll throughout Fernweh. I keep playing the instance over and over in my mind and cannot figure out what the Humble did wrong. I am surprised I thought of the shocking device. I would have not used it on Jack. Yelling seemed to suffice. Treating Jack like that came so naturally. I guess we have just had good training.

We come upon a cute coffee shop that has white rustic weathered doors. It is called The Muse. I turn to go in about to open the door. I catch myself and Jack rushes forward opening the door without hesitation.

There are a couple cute little blue tables scattered throughout. All the Masters sit and talk. Some of them are even laughing. It feels like a normal coffee shop that you would see in a movie. A place where friends would meet or where the main character would nervously wait for a blind date. I wonder if they do blind dates in Fernweh.

We walk up and I order a tall flat white. I am not sure what it is, but I see it written in all caps on the chalk board menu. I am about to ask Jack what he wants, and again I catch myself. We wait for a couple minutes, and I continue to glance around in awe of the cool abstract art on the walls and the feathered light fixtures hanging from the ceiling. It is so modern rustic, I love it. Maybe this will become my new favorite coffee shop. The idea sounds so grown up and chic. I am genuinely enjoying myself. I feel like an adult.

The man behind the counter, a Humble in bright turquoise blue that matches the tables gives me my coffee and smiles. I am about to take a seat when Jack lightly nudges me. A nudge if seen could be mistaken for an accidental bump, but I know he is trying to get my attention. I look around noticing that other than the man who served us coffee, there is not another Humble in sight. *Where are they?* I thought they couldn't leave their Master's side. *Why did I not notice that they weren't here?* The man behind the counter clears his throat and I make my way back over to him.

"My apologies Ma'am, as I am sure you are aware, there is a separate room for the Humbles behind that door." He points to a door to my left as he slightly glances me up and down conspicuously.

"Thank you, yes I knew that. I was just debating whether I wanted to take this to go or take a seat. I think we-I will take my coffee to go. Thank you." I smile and do an about-face turn and hurry out of the coffee shop opening the door myself with Jack trailing behind me. We will not be coming back to this coffee shop again. That was a close call.

We head back home to grab some food and we still have an hour left before our meeting with Elizabeth. I want to keep exploring. This is the first place I have ever been outside of our small town in Virginia. While it feels more like a weird dream than reality, excited adrenaline pumps through my veins.

"Jack, let's explore a little more before meeting our neighbor. Please?" I say smiling. This time my smile is not returned.

"Ella, you do not have to ask me. My opinion doesn't matter here, remember? You are the boss," he replies as he heads towards the door to open it for me. His response angers me. *Why was I asking for his permission anyway?* I am an adult.

I walk out with my head held high, as if that will salvage my pride and the embarrassment I just felt. We walk down the same route, but faster this time. I want to see what else Fernweh has in store for us.

As we walk out of the main suburb area, papaya trees are lined up perfectly to our left and right. Then it turns into a pineapple field, with the spiky leaves poking up through the red dirt. All the while the warm sun beats down and a tropical breeze blows every now and then to cool us off. The mountains jut out in the background, alternating navy, and light blue against the pale baby blue sky. One of the mountain tops is glowing red. A volcano waiting to erupt. It is beautiful.

I am distracted and barely notice the travelers becoming sparser. The navy-blue outfits continue to thin until I am the only Master walking, surrounded by bright turquoise, pink. yellow, and orange dirty shirts. Off in the distance the bright colors are not moving. *Are they staring at me? Why are they so still?* I start to feel uncomfortable, and a crawling feeling creeps up my back. I am outnumbered here. Without thinking, I reach down and grab Jack's hand. He pulls it away quickly then abruptly stops. I do the same, letting my eyes adjust.

The bright colors were not all moving because they are not all Humbles. As far as the eye can see there are piles and piles of trash. So much for the most environmentally friendly Earth.

The Humbles are rummaging through it, sleeping, sitting, and eating. This is their home. This is where the working Humbles live. I am in shock. I have never seen such unfortunate living circumstances before. Not in real life.

"I bring my Humble here sometimes to remind her how lucky she is", a sharp and even voice says behind me. I whirl around and there is a Master in a navy-blue dress displaying a perfect figure. She looks about in her thirties and her blue eyes are wide, round, and sparkle. I immediately recognize her but cannot pinpoint from where.

"I am Ella, nice to meet you", I say reaching out my hand. I try control it from shaking.

"I am Elizabeth, I know we said 2PM but I saw you leave for a walk, and I thought it was such a nice idea on a beautiful day like this. I truly did not mean to follow you; this is just my normal walking route." Her eyes twinkle as slight wrinkles accompany them.

"No worries, I am thrilled to meet you!" I reply with a smile.

"Good, me too." She looks at Jack her eyes narrowing. I can feel the hatred. She doesn't even know him. Her gaze then lands on me and does a quick up and down. She starts to turn away and walk back when she stops suddenly.

Over her shoulder she says, "and do not worry. I will not tell your little secret." The beautiful woman smirks at me as if she really does know everything.

Chapter 11

Faded Sunflowers

[Lindsey]

Knowing that Ella and Jack are in my hometown brings tears to my eyes. Not for the reasons you might think.

Fernweh is one of the most beautiful places; full of sunshine fresh fruit, guarded by the surrounding blue mountains. I miss the warm breeze. I miss being able to go outside and pull a fresh papaya from a tree and crack it open. The juice from fruit running down my chin.

The continuation facility let us bask in the sun and enjoy the pleasure of fresh fruit once a month. They would take us to the field just before the huge trash pit and we would enjoy ourselves for twenty minutes. Then the enjoyment would be once again sliced and whittled down by the tour of what our lives could be. We would walk through the working Humbles' potent stinky land to be reminded that being trained for a Master is a privilege. Reminded that there is still a class of people whom we were luckier and better than.

Throughout this tour, I would keep my eyes on Mount Ryan, and watch the orange glow. Sometimes I would pray he would bubble over and his thick hot red tongue would demolish this sad neglected stanched land. I would always smile at the thought that while our lives were completely controlled, Mount Ryan would always have the last say. His threats to overflow and fill the land was the one hope I always clung to. I bet he is still calmly sitting in his fury watching over the misery.

My favorite item in the facility was my cot. It was the only item I owned. It was yellowed fabric with faded sunflowers covering it.

When I arrived at Master Sam and Master Ally's, I was blown away by the two-story house. The marble floors looked as if their cold hard beauty was just freshly sliced. A red velvet staircase wrapped upward through the middle. The ceiling was encased in gold detailing of beautiful flowers. It took my breath away.

Then I was led to my room.

It was a small closet with a plain white cot. I could feel my nose tingle and the tears creep up to my eyes. It was not that I expected a marble floor room. I knew my place; it was the one thing I was conditioned to know. I just wanted my sunflowers. I wouldn't get a glance of nature for a while. I swallowed the lump in my throat and made my eyelids hold in the avalanche of tears trying to break through. From Master Ally's earnest glare, I could see that she was waiting for an excuse to give me a beating.

Soon she stopped looking and finding reasons to beat me. She did not follow the rule book and wrote one that was instead based on her mood. She never beat me in my human form. She kept me as a tiger most of the time. I would sometimes wonder if being a human was something I had imagined.

Master Sam was sent to check that I was in my room at night. He had kind eyes. The first time I turned myself back to a human without permission and he caught me, I was sure it would result in being painfully snapped back into my animal form.

"Just turn back before morning," he said with a sad smile. He stood there for a while looking at my human form in what almost seemed like awe.

"Thank you." It was the first time I had talked in six months.

As I got older, Master Sam would sometimes stay a while and talk before I turned back to my animal form. He would update me on politics and whatever gossip Master Ally complained about to him that day. He would also bring me books.

He taught me what the words meant and how to write them. These books helped me cope. I would get to escape into adventure stories. Looking back, I think he picked them deliberately. The underdog always won. He seemed to really care about me. When I turned twelve, Sam got me something he called a 'birthday gift'. I had never received one before. It was a mirror.

I was mainly kept in tiger form and in my room. My Masters hired a Humble to do the cooking and cleaning, Ester. I had not seen my reflection since peering into the pond behind the continuation facility.

"So, you can see how beautiful you are." Sam looked right at me. I took a deep breath, envisioning my frizzy hair and light brown eyes. I pulled up the mirror, opened my eyes, and the creature I saw made me gasp in fear. It was my same head surrounded by my frizzy hair, but with bright green catlike eyes. My mouth, open in shock, showed off pointy canine teeth.

"Thank you, Master Sam, for my gift." I watched as my lips moved up and down in the mirror.

"I'll leave you for the night." His eyebrows furrowed together. I could tell he was worried about the gift, so I smiled a reassuring smile looking directly at him rather than my atrocious reflection. "Do not let Ally see your gift. It is our little secret." His eyes crinkled up at the sides and he turned around and closed the door softly.

Once his footsteps had gone off into the distance, I changed back into my tiger form looking in the mirror. Back and forth I went from human to tiger, tiger to human. No matter how many times I switched, the bright green eyes and pointy teeth never changed.

My caramel brown eyes were gone forever and replaced by two hard evergreen mossy pupils. I sat down and sobbed for the first time next to my plain white cot. I wondered if one day I would lose my human form altogether and be forever stuck in an animal's body.

That is why since I have arrived on Global Earth I have vowed to not transform ever again.

Chapter 12

Dinner

~ Ella ~

Jack and I have been in Fernweh for three days and I love it. I know I should not. It is bright, colorful, and for once in my life I have a purpose. It is weird looking like a bunch of strangers, but this is what I have always wanted, right?

I have always looked the part with my blonde hair and blue eyes; I have just never known the rules. Now I do and I have already made a friend. Elizabeth has invited us over for dinner. Unfortunately, she is the owner of the factory we have been sent to infiltrate. Lindsey said that it was pure chance that they were able to locate her before our journey started. Fate. I know I should not be this excited since my mission is essentially to betray her, but I am.

Jack is miserable.

He refuses to sleep in the spare bedroom. He curls up on his plain white cot. When we walk throughout the town and I find something amusing or weird, I instinctively look at him for confirmation. He never glances up from the ground. When we speak to people on the street, he stays silent. I am entitled to opinions and emotions, and he is not. He even plays his role in our house.

I know they instructed us to, but I want him back. His silence and avoiding eye contact just makes me want to look into his eyes even more. I keep having dreams where we kiss, then he shrieks, transforming into his deer form before disappearing. Last night he sat my dinner on the table and started to walk away to eat his in the kitchen. I grabbed his hand.

"Eat with me tonight, please." He did not pull away. His warm hand was in mine.

"Ella, we just need to play our parts so we can complete our mission and leave." He was staring right at me. I could feel the energy between us. Suddenly he glanced up, pulled his hand away, and quickly went into the other room. He has not talked, looked, or even acknowledged I exist all day. This is how we have arrived at Elizabeth's house; distant and disconnected.

Her house is magnificent. It is made of marble and looks as if it should have its own kingdom to rule over. Instead, it is sandwiched between our brick mansion and a cherry wood three story house. I take a deep breath before I lift the loop hanging out of a tiger's mouth on the door and let it drop.

"Good evening and welcome to my home." Elizabeth's voice rings out as the grand door swings open. It is as if she has been standing there just waiting for us to come. Maybe she doesn't have many friends either.

"Thank you so much for having us!" This is the first time in my life I have been invited over to someone's house for dinner. However, I cannot help but think of our first introduction when she said, "I will not tell your little secret". *What does this beautiful mysterious woman know?*

Ester walks out from behind the front door she just opened. She is a slender, pale woman who seems to be in her forties. It is very odd to have a Humble with a familiar that is older than a Master. She is a very unnerved woman whose hands are shaking just as they were when we met near the trash pile.

Elizabeth once again seems to read my mind.

"Ester is like family. She raised me after my parent's accident." She looks away afterward, which I interpret to mean she does not want to talk about 'the accident'.

"You have a beautiful home", I say in response, and I mean it. The marble on the outside continues inside, covering the floors and walls. It is not like the marble tile in our home. It is actual solid chunks of marble making up the walls. The glossy white, with wisps of grey, is interrupted by a red velvet staircase leading up to a painting of a woman with a dead tiger draped over her shoulders. The woman is obviously a Master and has Elizabeth's round eyes but without the sparkle.

"That painting was made in honor of my mother. It was a gift to me from the idiot detective assigned to her case." Elizabeth is staring at me as she says this, and I cannot tell what reaction she wants.

"Beautiful", repeating my previous observation.

I move my gaze up towards the ceiling. Gold swirls above make delicate flowers and leaves. It is not painted. Actual thin gold traces across the entire ceiling and shimmers in the light as my eyes scan. It is the most splendid sky I have ever seen.

"My parents built this house. They were very wealthy. They opened the shoe factory on 6th street, which now I own and manage. I have been looking to employ a Master to keep an eye on it for me, as it is very tiring work to check in on that dreadful, stinky building twice a week." She rolls her eyes to the back of her head reminding me of a typical bratty popular girl in a high school movie.

She leads us into the dining room and motions for me to sit as she describes how her parents came up with the idea of the shoe factory. She talks of how they hated that Humbles lived in trash and that they would create jobs for them and give them a purpose. She speaks of this all in a dreamy manner, painting the terrifying woman from the painting as a saint. I am not sure which to believe, concluding they both must be true.

I glance behind me to check on Jack. He is awkwardly standing by the archway into the dining room. I realize I have not instructed him on where to go. *Where should he go?* I start turning the training on etiquette over in my mind. *What did it say about visiting a guest house?* Nothing.

Elizabeth interrupts my panicked thoughts.

"Jack you are welcome to sit at the other end of the table if Ella approves. Ester will join you." Elizabeth looks at me with her sparkling eyes. I cannot tell if this is a sincere invitation or a test. I glance at Jack for a split second hoping his eyes will have the answer. He is looking at the ground.

"Jack you may join if that is what our kind hostess prefers", I respond without a tremor of nervousness in my voice. I am proud of this response. I am so clever.

"Where are you from? It seems you just appeared here", Elizabeth asks as Ester brings out a beautiful fruit salad.

"We are from Zugzwang, the town about 15 miles west of Fernweh. My parents passed away and as you know Zugzwang can be quite industrialized. I wanted the warmth of Fernweh," I repeat the scripted answer that I practiced many times in training hoping it sounds like a fact and not a line from a play.

"You meant to say, 'I am from Zugzwang'." Elizabeth responds with her round eyes narrowed.

"Yes, is that not what I said?" I reply pushing my eyebrows up and together like a house to mirror confusion. *How could I have possibly messed this up already?*

"Oh, I thought you said 'we' when we both know Jack is truly from Fernweh. Fernweh's continuation facility is something we Fernwehians are all proud of. We supply the world with labor." She says this with a smile on her face as if it is the most wonderful fact she knows.

"Of course. This salad is delicious." I smile and take my first bite. My face is churning as if hot lava is underneath my smooth skin. *Congrats on producing a bunch of slaves and servants* I sarcastically think.

"However, as time goes on, we have realized the importance of smart breeding and proper selection of familiars." She is looking off in the distance as if my comment were not even heard. "I started the 'no predators' campaign after the birthing facility faculty who approved of my parent's familiar was charged. I also pressed charges against the Humbles who were responsible for birthing that little creature. They were executed. Thanks to me, Masters are safe."

Her eyes lock with mine on the last line causing a chill to shoot through my back. Ester sits bloody rare steaks on the table and my stomach flips. "That is why I was assigned Ester. Her familiar is a lamb. She has watched over me since the accident when I was 8." Blood drips down her delicate chin as she bites into the steak. I look over and Ester sits a bowl of oatmeal in front of Jack, and they eat side by side with their heads down.

"I am terribly sorry about the accident and that your parent's safety was compromised." I look at her hoping she will reveal more of her tragedy with me. True friends reveal the things that hurt the most. *"She is not your friend, nor will she ever be Ella. Focus on the mission."* Lindsey's voice rings through my head, she sounds irritated. I feel myself stiffen and Elizabeth notices.

"Ester, Jack, please go start on dishes", Elizabeth commands keeping her eyes on me. Once they exit into the kitchen, her bright eyes dim.

"Listen to me", she says in a quick and dark whisper, "I saw you reach for Jack's hand through the window last night. I know it is hard being alone and I understand. But if anyone else would have seen that, they would report you to the court to be under watch. There is no tolerance for that behavior here. I have never been to Zugzwang, but here it will get you killed. I have been interviewed for it before and I have no problem telling the truth. I am a nice person, so I will not turn you in. Beware of weakness. Not only within others, within yourself. This is how you will protect yourself here. Now, you are not weak, are you?" I feel white hot creep over my face, hoping the paleness is actualizing only under my skin.

"Of course not", I respond fiercely. I feel embarrassed like a scolded child.

"It is horrible how they are treated, but Ella we have the upper hand for a reason. I mean, they are the animal we assign to them. They are all inherently weak because we made them that way. Do not let the less-than or weak rule." She sips her red wine as if everything she has said to me is a simple fact.

Lindsey is right: this woman will never be my friend.

"Well thank you so much for dinner! I would love to talk about that position you mentioned in the factory, if you would like? Just let me know. It is time I turn in for the night." I smile at her the warmest smile I can muster, given the circumstances. "Jack! It is time to leave come now!" I scream loudly, as if he is miles away. Elizabeth follows us to the door and pulls me in for a hug.

"We are going to be remarkably close friends! I would love to see you at dinner tomorrow. Let's do your place!" Her eyes have their sparkle once again, as if our conversation had not just happened.

As Jack and I walk back to our home, I can feel her eyes following us. When we step inside, I look at Jack.

"We need to close all our blinds", I say finding I am angry. *Is that why he pulled away? Why wouldn't he tell me she saw us?* He just left me out for the wolves in there. "Why didn't you tell me you saw her Jack? We could be killed. Do you understand?" I am yelling and holding on to his arm tight.

"Yeah, well maybe you should not hold my hand, look at me like you do, and invite me to sleep in a fluffy bed, Ella. Do not act like I am the one to blame. This is not our world. We are just playing our parts so we can leave. You act like you just moved to a new city and this is life. It is not, Ella. You do not fit in here. You do not have friends. You have a part to play and people to save." He rips his arm from my grip and goes to close all the blinds.

I want to cry. I am alone. I hate to admit it, but he and Lindsey are right, I need to focus.

Chapter 13

My Other ¼
JACK

Susan was right about Ella, she is in it for herself. She likes the control and power.

She is not the girl I use to sit next to in front of the brick wall. That anger and rage she has always had churning under the surface is going to blow at some point. It will be pointed at me. She acts like she doesn't have the heart to do it. She does. I saw her eyes glaze over in training. I saw her get more and more use to watching me painfully contort. Which is why Susan and I's plan has changed.

It is the middle of the night, and I am on my way to meet myself. The Perfect Earth version of myself. Originally, I was to be the sacrifice and when I died, he would build on the knowledge I shared. Or at least that is what we told him. Now I need to convince him to take the fall. He does not know what is coming.

This is taking self-manipulation to a whole new level.

The streets are quiet, and our meeting spot is a good walk away. We're meeting where there are no cameras. I walk past the colorful trash, by people sleeping behind cardboard and blanket walls. Some eyes peer out at me wondering. Children who can't sleep, mothers who worry about their babies' ribs poking out, fathers who are too drunk to fully sit up, the eyes of these people who are relying on me to really set this world straight. They just do not know it yet.

As I walk deeper, the trash gets thicker, and the smell encapsulates my body. I hold back a gag.

Eventually, I arrive at the bottom of the volcano, the glow leading me the whole way. There through two trees, I see a hut. It isn't built out of blankets and cardboard like the other homes. It has actual wooden walls, and the roof is made of tree branches. It looks like a boho playhouse that a rich person would buy their child.

I start to walk towards the door and pause. Sharon warned me that Jack and I cannot simultaneously exist within one dimension for too long. That is why we can't let our plan drone out. I must make sure the Jack of this earth understands the urgency. He knows a lot about what needs to happen here, but he doesn't know of the alternate realities like I do. I have been trained.

I take a deep breath and walk to the door. Before I have the chance to knock with my trembling fist, the door swings open. My mouth drops and goes dry. I stare at myself. He stares back at me. He looks just like my reflection, but he is smiling.
He looks…..happy.

"Hey I am Jack", I say reaching out my hand. He starts laughing a deep belly laugh that is layered with years of practice. I am immediately jealous.

"Me too bud. I am not going to shake your hand though. The less contact we have, the better." He smirks at me. Maybe he knows more about the alternate realities than we thought.

"So what brings ya to Jack's shack?", he says with yet another smile. He doesn't seem like me at all. I know we have had different lives and paths, I just assumed he would think my thoughts and be well I guess, me.

"Thank you for welcoming me.", I sputter out awkwardly. I wait for him to respond but he just stands in his doorway patiently waiting for me to continue. He still has not invited me in. "I just wanted to come meet you and solidify some things about our plan." He better not make this difficult.

"Well, I would love to gab and have a sleep over, but kid we need to limit our contact. I know you're new to all this, but I am not. If we keep sharing the same breathing air, we are going to create a bigger problem than the one we are tryin' to beat. You understand, bud?" He lowers his head, and his golden-brown eyes turn dark. Just like mine do when I am upset.

I do not like that he calls me kid. We are the same age. Hell, we are the same person.

"Yes I got it. What do you mean you aren't new to this?" I ask curt, curious if he has traveled to one of the other dimensions. I feel like I barely know what is happening now. I expected him to be simple and more like a clone of myself. He is a separate person that has just stolen my body.

"Like I said kid, no time to gab. What do you want?" He does not smile this time.

"The plan has changed. I am not doing too well separating myself from my partner so it would be better if you and I switched spots now. The hammer will be falling soon, and I want to make sure things go according to plan." I shift my weight back and forth to come off as the nervous kid I know he views me as. Maybe if I act like the innocent kid, he has conjured in his mind he will give me grace.

"Ahhh I get it. You have a boner for the little lady you're with and can't keep focused. Ya'll want me to go in and do all the heavy lifting. By the hammer, I assume you want me to end up in front of the jury and want me to end up in a pile of bodies so you can gain my knowledge and keep going to meet the other Jack's. Do I got it right?" He is smiling but I can feel the anger. I stay silent.

"Look kid, this is my plan. Not yours. You are part of my mission, my life, MY plan. So, you are not going to come in here and change all the rules. I know you think we are equals but I know things you could never understand. I have been through much worse than your sad lonely life. So, buck up and do your job. Got it?"

"Look I am sorry to offend but this is not your plan, it is our plan. I have prepared my whole life to watch it all burn. You are not going to take that away from me." I spit back. He looks up and squints as if studying my brain inside my head.

Silence hangs in the air.

I take a deep breath. "How about a compromise?"

He looks to the side and taps his foot nervously. I almost smile. I do the same thing when I want to seem anxious. I wonder if he wants to seem anxious or is anxious.

"Okay, what you mean by compromise?", he finally says.

"What if we both live? What if we help each other out? Right before the agency captures me, let's switch. I will make sure to get you out and we burn it to the ground together." I say this consciously making sure my foot stays still. I hope he doesn't see through this lie.

"You are right, why can't we both live?", he says with the bright smile he greeted me with. His sudden mood change makes me nervous. "In the end lets meet back here at Jack's shack sound like a plan?".

"So, you will come switch with me before the agency takes me?", I ask.

"I promise ya Jack, we will both live. I got friends in high places." He says with a wink. I do not know what this means or if I should believe him.

"Gentlemen's agreement?", I quietly say with an outstretched hand. He starts laughing once again. That same happy laugh makes me grit my teeth together. If he has been through so much worse, how come he has that laugh?

"Boy if I didn't know better, I would say you are trying to break the universe! Gentlemen's agreement, but like I said. I am not touching your hand." He continues to laugh as I awkwardly lower my outstretched hand to my side for the second time in our conversation. I wish he would've grabbed it.

"It's been nice meeting you Jack." I say sounding relieved. I don't know why, but I truly feel like he will come through for me.

"Yeah, you too, and don't worry. I got you." He nods his head. Right then and there I know the next time we see each other it will be through a cloud of smoke. We will win. I turn to go back home.

"Wait, if you ever need any medicine or anything stop on by. I got everything you could possibly need alright?" He yells out as I walk away. I smile and wave in acknowledgement still trying to process what just happened.

He is so charming and so unlike me.

Chapter 14

Hostess
~ Ella ~

To prepare for a dinner guest is not a task I have ever imagined myself doing. Especially a guest as sweetly terrifying as Elizabeth.

I have barked orders at Jack all day as I, myself, have helped complete them. Clean the windowsills, dust the mantle, and vacuum the couch. My body has nervous jitters, as if I drank too much coffee. I have not eaten or had anything to drink all day. As the time approaches for our expected guest, I sit my shaky mess of nerves down on a chair near the door.

Jack has lamb prepared and a fresh fruit salad. The food aromas are making my stomach grumble. I peek through the shades and see her perfect figure shifting left and right towards our house, followed by poor, slim, and worn Ester. I try to imagine Ester as an animal and cannot. *What is her familiar?* I can't remember.

I fling open the door abruptly, forgetting that Jack is supposed to do this part, and say, "Welcome to my home."

"Why thank you for having me, Ella. This house is beautiful. I have always wanted a peek inside. There was a rumor that it is owned by the agency." Her smile is radiant, but my mind is stuck on 'owned by the agency'. I know I should let it go but I ask anyway.

"What do you mean 'owned by the agency?'" I ask, trying to sound more generally curious than truly worried.

"Well people have said that it is owned by The Agency Board, Fernweh's sector of government. It is probably only a rumor, but no one has lived in this house since the judge who mysteriously died 10 years ago. People said that he had relations with his Humble, and that the agency found out. He was never seen again."

I can feel my face turn hot white. *Why would Steve put us in this house? What if there are hidden cameras?*

"It is probably all just talk. Besides, you have nothing to worry about, right?" Elizabeth flashes her pearly whites and her sparkling blue eyes widen, waiting my response.

"Right, well let me show you around! Ester you can join Jack in the kitchen." I motion towards the stairs and show her through the spectacular house, all the while keeping my eye out for possible hidden cameras.

As we sit down for our delicious dinner, Elizabeth abruptly says, "I want you to manage my shoe factory." She immediately blushes, as if she has just told a secret.

"Really? Wow thank you for the opportunity! I would love that." I beam. I expected this part to take much longer. Now I am in.

All I need to do is figure how to get 200 Humbles to the safe land. Elizabeth is now intently trying to peel my face away, to view my brain with her eyes. They scream 'what is she thinking?' I feel the need to say more but cannot think of any words. I am too busy planning.

"I will bring you by tomorrow and show you around and introduce the Humbles." I am so thankful she has broken the silence.

"I am so glad we have come into each other's lives. I feel like I can truly trust you." She continues to stare.

"I feel like I can trust you too and I am looking forward to starting this adventure with you." I smile but have a feeling deep down that we are both lying. I know why I am, but why is she?

Jack comes out and sits the lamb dressed in mint on the table. Elizabeth's stare moves to her plate. She turns pale and for a moment I think she might pass out.

"Elizabeth are you alright?" I ask.

She looks up nervously. "I am fine. I apologize to be rude, but I do not eat lamb." She glances quickly out of the corner of her eye to Ester. An awkward and appreciative smile spreads across Ester's delicate face. It disappears as quickly as it showed up that for a moment, I think I imagined it. It was a sweet, pure, and genuine as a ripple in the water.

Then I realize what made Elizabeth so queasy. Ester's familiar is a lamb. My face burns hot with embarrassment and disgust. My appetite vanishes and my grumbling stomach tightens.

"Elizabeth……Ester, I am so sorry. I did not realize….." I awkwardly throw out into the still room.

"Apologize for what? I just have a little indigestion is all. We better get going. Thank you for having us and I will see you at the factory tomorrow." Elizabeth shoots back and flashes a fake smile.

I kindly escort her and Ester out of my house apologizing as I do. I shut the door behind me and turn around and stare at the lamb in disgust.

Exhaustion bounces over me like a rubber band that has been held taught and was just let go. I hate being a hostess, especially when you are skating on thin ice above an ocean of tension. Jack enters the room with a smirk on his face as he picks up the plates of lamb.

"Nice move, trying to make our guest a cannibal." He looks at me waiting for a laugh or a smile. I can't. That all felt off. Not just the food. Not just the comment regarding the agency.

"Jack, it feels too easy. She is hiding something, and I just do not feel right about this. Also, why would Steve put us in a house owned by the Agency?" I pace back and forth trying to dissect the past thirty minutes looking for a sign. A clue. *What is she up to?*

"Ella, maybe you are just projecting your feelings on her. You are the one hiding quite a deal. Besides, so what if she is hiding something? This is what we came here for. We got an in and we can be out of here in a week and back to our normal lives.

As far as the house, I think Elizabeth suspects we have a romantic relationship. She probably just made that up to see your reaction. She has been prodding you with jabs about us since the beginning. Ella, there is nothing romantic between us, so we have nothing to worry about." He is talking louder and more excited than he has since we have begun this whole journey.

I feel anger bubbling inside of me. 'We' he had said. But I am the one smiling, faking, and figuring out the plan. He just follows me around moping and sleeping on his tiny cot. A lump grows in my throat as I mull over the words 'there is nothing romantic between us'. I guess I did make it all up. I feel embarrassment rise to my cheeks being pushed with an undercurrent of resentment and anger.

"It might take longer than a week." I say this through gritted teeth.

"Why? Ella, come on, we got this. I want to go home. I am miserable." His eyes are pleading for me to say I agree. I do not.

"Because, Jack, we cannot just waltz in and free 200 people. We must build relationships and rapport and get out without being killed. This is not something we rush. Besides, I do not know why you are so miserable. I do all the work; you just follow me around. It's not like it will be any better for you at home anyways." I immediately wish I could grab the words and shove them back down my throat. Tears well up in his eyes.

"Ella, that is not my choice. It is my role. I do not just follow you around. I make all your food, clean, and follow every demand. I eat on the floor and sleep on a paper-thin cot. My whole-body aches and my mind is turned off. I just go through the motions, because if I think about it too much I will break. None of this is the worst part.

The worst part is that you enjoy it. You enjoy bossing me around. You enjoy the power. Maybe that is why it will take longer than a week, Ella. Maybe you do not want to leave because you know in our world no one cares about who you are, and no one listens. Maybe back home is not that bad compared to being your slave!" Now he is yelling, and tears stream down his face.

"If you really think that is who I am, then you are wrong. No one listens to me in our world, but I thought you did. I am just trying to be careful and not get us killed. Bossing you around is my role too."

The tears start to well up. I let them overflow and bite my lip. I start to storm out of the kitchen then catch myself standing still in the doorway. "By the way, we need to search the house for hidden cameras." I wait for a response. I wait for Jack to come put his arms around me and tell me he did not mean anything he said. I wait for him to apologize. Silence fills the room.

I went too far; I shouldn't have taken such a low blow about home. I do not look back and walk out, knowing I will not be able to sleep with this in the air.

Chapter 15

Magic Shoes
~*Ella* ~

The air is warm, with a breeze blowing through the windows of our vintage car. Jack's eyes are smiling as he weaves us through traffic. It is the first time I have seen his eyes look that bright and free of storms in a while. I want to reach out and grab his hand and tell him I am sorry that I order him around. I want to tell him he is right; I do like the power. I want to tell him he is right; I am a horrible person.

Instead, I smile lightly and continue to look out of the back seat window as navy blue and flashes of neon colors whisk by. As we drive further, the white houses are separated by brick buildings in the industrial part of Fernweh.

We pull up to a tall, dirty, brick building with a giant red pump shoe on the top. It looks very rustic.

It is not at all what I expected Elizabeth to oversee. I was expecting sparkling white and clean, with drops of blue incorporated. As we pull up to the curb in front of the building, a Humble cowers over to valet our vehicle. He shakes Jacks hand and avoids eye contact with me, smiling in my direction. The double doors framed in industrial rusted silver swing open, and the smell of leather and glue hits my nostrils. This is the same smell I notice when I start to wake up from a dream and I wait. I wait for the lavender puree to rescue me.

A pang of wanting to be home punches my gut for the first time.

Elizabeth enters in a navy-blue pant suit with a paisley blue scarf woven through her brown hair. She is beaming with excitement and says, "Welcome! Oh, Ella I am so glad you are interested in this opportunity. This place needs so much work, but I just do not have enough time on my hands with all the initiatives I am a part of." She brings her shoulders up to her ears and drops them violently with a dramatic sigh.

"Of course, getting involved in a business I care about is why I came here," I say. She nods and starts walking quickly away, motioning for me to follow. She leads Jack and I to a silver rusted elevator and we start on the fifth floor.

The smell of plastic fills the air as the elevator doors open. There is a glass room in the back with a giant machine and a hologram of a tennis shoe is shown hovering above a table. Three Humbles wearing brown shirts huddle around it. They glance quickly, noticing our arrival, and nervously disperse. A long silver rectangle is coming out of the side of the glass room, making a humming noise, and goes down into the floor. There are 10 tables, each with a Humble sketching, entering in dimensions onto the screen on the table, or frantically typing what looks like coding jargon.

"This is our design team. They research and draw up the style and dimensions of each shoe that exists in Fernweh. They also create a shoe 'last.' The 'last' replicates the foot that will go into the shoe. That is digitally printed and sent to the shoe room on the first floor."

Elizabeth talks quickly, as if this is a review session before a test. I realize I know nothing about how shoes are made.

"Why are all the Humbles wearing brown?" I ask, genuinely curious why they are not sporting the common bright colors.

"That is their uniform. It is a reminder that they are part of this factory, and this is where their allegiance lies. The color blends in with the brick wall, don't you agree?" She smiles as if this is a positive sentiment and does not wait for my answer. "Now let's make our way to the sewing and stamping floor."

The elevator doors close us in a cube of awkward silence. They open with a screech as flakes of rust fall. The smell of leather, oil, and glue punches us in the face once again, making me feel queasy for a moment.

There are huge machines the size of monster trucks that Humbles are feeding leather into, while from the sides, shoes come out. There are ten of these giant machines throughout the fourth floor.

"This is the stamping and sewing room. The machines do most of the work, so there is no need for breaks. I will give you a further break-down of how the machines work and which feeds into which when you officially agree to take this on." Elizabeth scans the room with narrowed eyes that remind me of the woman holding the dead tiger in the painting above her velvet stairs. It makes my skin crawl.

I have the feeling she is on her best behavior due to Jack and my presence.

We enter the third floor next and, like the fourth floor, it smells of oil and leather. The sound of soft gun shots is heard across the room and 10 of the biggest staple machines I have ever seen stand before me. Humbles stand, running the leather and cotton cut outs from the previous floor into a machine that shapes them and pounds staples into the sole.

"This is the shoe assembly floor. This is where the shoes are put together in complete form. The next floor is my favorite", she says with a wistful look.

That is when I realize this is all she has of her parents. This is hers and she wants to give this baby to me. Out of all the gifts and trinkets I have ever been given, this one has true sentimental value. Possibly more than James, my metal protector. I feel my throat catch. Lindsey enters my head whispering, *'Ella, concentrate on the mission. She is using you, just as you are using her.'*

I swallow the emotion down like a shot. It burns worse than the vodka I drank from my parent's liquor cabinet. I quickly blink three times to subdue any possible tears, which surprises me. I have not thought of my parents since this journey started. I wonder if they have thought of me. They probably have not even noticed I am gone.

The second floor has barely any machines, except the one that feeds the complete shoes from the previous floors. There are about 30 tables with holographic prints hovering above them. Humbles are pushing around carts, trading out sharp knives, and what looks like a cheese slicer.

Other Humbles are sitting at the tables, entering, and selecting shoe images that float into the middle of the digital design. Then a red light is scanned across the shoe, and it comes out the side of the table with designs in the leather. The Humbles then pick up the freshly imprinted shoe and whittle away, tweaking the designs.

I have never seen anything like it. I wonder if we have technology like this on our earth. It is how I have always imagined Santa's toy shop. Except it looks as if someone painted everything brown and orange.

"This is our insoles and decorations department. The designs are sent from the fifth floor, and they are punched into the shoe and insoles inserted. This team is responsible for the perfection of each design. Any design issue falls on them to fix. This floor has some of the most skilled people in this factory. They get one ten-minute break for every 8-hour shift." I want to ask about their lunch breaks and where they eat but decide to wait till the end of the tour.

We are about to leave when two Humbles come in from the elevator. I freeze in my tracks.

The woman is skinny, with hallowed cheeks and a curved back; she is a dirty, sad, unpolished version of my mother. *She is my mother.* I want to ask her what she is doing here. I am about to open my mouth when I feel Jack slightly pinch me.

"What the hell are you doing not working on your floor and using our elevator?!" Elizabeth screams.

Only then do I realize a man is standing beside her. They are holding hands, but it is not my father. This is not my mother. This is Perfect Earth's version of her. I cannot believe my mother is here. My beautiful perfect movie star mother is a dirty servant who makes shoes. Part of me wants to laugh in her face but a bigger part wants to hug her.

"I'm sorry ma'am, James and I needed water," my mom says, looking at the floor in a voice that is muddled.

James.

My middle name.

I try to process what this could mean. I want to ask a billion questions. Instead, I inch closer to Jack.

"Since we have guests, I will let this go. However, missy, understand this: if I catch any unwarranted breaks happening again, you will both go in front of the jury." Elizabeth spits out these words into my mother's face.

I want to punch her.

I want to rip her perfect chestnut hair out of her perfectly shaped head.

Elizabeth looks at me embarrassed. "I know, Ella, this behavior angers me just as much as it angers you. When you work here, you will unfortunately have to deal with imbeciles such as these two." She rolls her eyes and walks towards the elevator.

I pause and stare into my mother's eyes. She quickly looks down. She has no idea who I am. A sting hits the tip of my nose and travels up to my eyes. It's heartbreaking to be forgotten. It is even more heartbreaking to realize you've never been known by someone you love so dearly.

To her, I am just another rich lady that could get her in trouble, or worse, killed. Jack nudges me to move and I spring forward almost running to the elevator.

The first floor is lined with shelves, and shoes constantly appear on the shelves, as if by magic. In the back of the room the shoe lasts from the fifth floor are being put into different shoes by Humbles. There is also a shining table, where Humbles place shoes into boxes and put the boxes on a belt that takes them out of the room.

"This is the Shoe Room. This is where the shoes are inspected, and the dimensions are checked and compared to the shoe last created on the fifth floor. They are then pushed out to the back room where the addresses are pressed on them, and we have drones deliver them."

"Weird. I have not seen any drones. Also, where do the Humbles take lunch?" I say. Elizabeth cocks her head to one side, as if she is a confused puppy.

"Take lunch? We are not responsible for their eating habits. Coming from Zugzwang I am surprised by this question."

"Oh, my apologies. I meant, where do I take lunch? Not them." I smile and place my hands behind my back, due to them shaking from fear she will see through this recovery.

"Silly me, I must have heard incorrectly! Yes, your office is this way. Feel free to go out for lunch." We are led to the lobby of the building, through a glass tunnel with blooming flowers growing around it and the sun glittering through.

We enter a blue room that is crystal clean and nothing like the rusting building we just toured. "This is my office and will become yours once you take over. Isn't it cute?" She smiles, reminding me of a small child. I smile just in case she glances over.

She then leads us outside and to the very back of the building. There are two trees with a brown wooden shack built in between them. We enter and the smell of trash and sweat fills the air. Elizabeth holds her nose and has her leather gloves on. I put mine on, understanding that we are in an 'unclean' area.

"I apologize; I will get them to clean this up. They are so disgusting." She rolls her eyes. "This is the Humbles' dressing room. The entrance is in the back." I look and see no door on the back wall, so I walk forward, and my step becomes hollow.

There it is: our entrance into the Humbles' underground world. I try to look as if I am just looking around to hide my exciting discovery. I can feel Jack's excitement beside me and quickly glare at him to control himself.

"I would be honored to manage this factory. Are there any certain rules you have for me?" I say this truly unsure of what my responsibilities are, hoping she will explain them.

"Really? Oh, thank you Ella! You will just need to check in on this place three times a week, for as long or as little as you would like, just to make sure everything is functioning. I will introduce you to Bert and Henry. Bert works days and Henry works nights. They unofficially oversee the place."

"That is interesting that you have Humbles in charge. That's very progressive of you." I say with a smile hoping this gets under her skin.

She is unfazed.

"You know how it is, everyone has Humbles do their dirty work. We have no other choice." She looks at the silver watch on her wrist, surrounded by diamonds. "I have to be at the continuation facility for a board meeting! I will catch up with you later. Call with any questions." She briskly walks out, almost skipping, as if she is going to meet a secret lover.

So that is her true baby: the board of the continuation facility. This is her secondary gig. That makes this whole situation easier. I smile at Jack.

"We are in", I say gleefully. Jack opens his mouth, about to respond, then quickly looks down. I slowly turn around to see two men wearing bright red standing behind me.

"You must be Bert and Henry." I extend my hand, but make sure I do not smile. I do not know how loyal Bert and Henry are to Elizabeth. I am hoping their allegiance lies with their own people, but their scowls tell me a different story.

Chapter 16

Lizzy

[Lindsey]

I remember the day Master Ally came home with Lizzy.

In my closet of a room, I heard screaming. I creaked my door and laid my eyes on the girl who would steal my heart. She looked upset to have entered this world and was the most stunning thing I had ever seen.

"Please, someone take this screaming child. I had to push her out of me, do not think for one second, I am going to put up with this as well. I need sleep." She let go and I quickly rushed out of my room catching the ball of fury in my hands just in time.

Lizzy stopped crying and her tiny hand squeezed my finger reminding me of my fury friend with the black eyes from the continuation facility. It was the first time I had ever felt love for another human.

From that day on, I was Lizzy's second mother. I bathed her, fed her, told her stories, and loved her with all my heart. I taught her that Humbles are people too. I told her over and over that she could change the world and show people that everyone matters. I wanted her to be strong, kind, and good, despite her parents and the friends she would make. I wanted her to treat her Humble as an equal, not as a slave. Maybe by the time she was old enough to own a Humble, there would be none to own, just people. What if she could bring this change?

She could barely talk as I preached this into her head, but I hope that some of it stuck. She had the brightest blue eyes ever seen in any Master. They were full of wonder, excitement, and potential. A smile from her could make any shocking feel worth it.

When Lizzy turned three, Master Ally decided it was time to be a mother. I started seeing Lizzy less and less. I was a tiger more and more. Lizzy began to learn her place in society and what it meant. She went to social gatherings with her mother, wearing dresses full of frills and navy-blue bows on the top of her head.

When she was four years old, she gave me her first command.

"Get me juice! Now!" she yelled, her sparkling eyes dimming for the first time. It was worse than any beating or transformation I had ever received from Master Ally.

Tears welled up in my eyes as I went to the kitchen. I came back with her juice and handed it to her looking at the floor. "Lindy?" She asked with concern. Hearing her sweet voice still not able to pronounce my name was unbearable. My sweet girl was slipping between my fingers. I kept my eyes on the floor and went back into the kitchen and cried for the second time in my life.

Lizzy told Master Ally about my behavior, and I received one of the worst beatings yet. Master Ally made Lizzy watch.

I could not move from my cot for two days. The second day, while I was feeling sore and defeated, a slight knock came from the other side of my matchbox coffin of a room. Expecting Master Sam, I slowly made myself sit up.

Lizzy's small voice chimed nervously on the other side of the door, "Lindy, I come in?"

"Yes of course, Lizzy," my voice croaked. And there she was, my innocent, kind Lizzy.

"I'm sorry." She tried to say something more, but tears welled up and started to splatter on the floor.

"Do not cry Lizzy, it is not your fault. Come here." She came over and I held her and told her I loved her. I told her she gets to choose who she is. I told her she is not her mother.

"I want to be like you, Lindy." She looked up smiling, her blue eyes looking vibrant against the red watery white surrounding her pupils.

"You have the opportunity to be nothing like me. You have power and a say." She looked confused and I knew she was too young to understand this. I hoped she would, one day.

I took her to the bathroom and brushed her beautiful chestnut hair. I took a blow dryer, dried the tear-soaked neckline, and gently spread moisturizer across her face. I knew my body could not handle another beating, not that day. She led me back to my room and told me she was going to talk to the kitchen Humble.

"Lindy, mom says you call me Elizabeth. Lizzy is not for a Master name." She smiled her innocent smile and gently shut the door.

My heart fluttered with disappointment, and I vowed to call her Lizzy whenever Master Ally was not around.

That I did.

Lizzy started to rebel when she was five years old. She argued with teachers in school about why there were not any Humbles in her class. She yelled at her mom when they would make me eat on the floor in public. She told all her friends to call her Lizzy and rolled her eyes at Master Ally when she was scolded.

All of this resulted in my body being constantly covered in bruises for Lizzy's actions. I took it in stride and did not shed one tear. I was proud of Lizzy. I just knew she was going to be different. I just knew she was going to change the world. I taught her to be better somehow and was so proud of myself for that.

Then, as everything in life, it backfired.

Lizzy came home from school one day with a Humble. He was a blonde boy with big brown eyes. He looked about nine years old. I met her at the door and was at a loss for words when I saw her friend. I was glowing inside with joy for how brave she was being.

"Elizabeth, why do you have that thing in my house?" Master Ally's shrill voice rang through the foyer. A chill traveled its way down my back, and I stepped aside.

"This is my friend. His name is Bobby." Elizabeth beamed. "I snuck him away from Mrs. Snikerson." She was proud.

I was scared.

This was the day I was going to be beat to death.

"Snuck him away? Elizabeth, this behavior has gotten out of hand. You are going to be punished for this, you understand?" Master Ally's voice was quick and hard. Her face was beat red, with her nostrils flaring in and out. Little Lizzy's face went white with fear. Her mother had never threatened her before. She had never faced consequences for her actions. I had always paid her dues.

Master Ally was talking on the phone with Mrs. Snikerson, assuring her that she would issue punishment to her daughter. She came back and led Lizzy and the terrified Humble boy into the sitting room. She would not make eye contact with either of them. We all sat in silence until Mrs. Snikerson arrived. Mrs. Snikerson apologized, seizing the boy from the ground by his ears and causing him to whimper. She said it would not happen again.

Once they exited the house, Master Ally towered over her daughter.

"Master Ally, it is my fault Elizabeth does not understand--", Ally slapped me across the face so hard it brought me to my knees and my head started to ring.

"Be quiet! This is *my* daughter, not yours. I will do with her whatever the hell I please!" She yelled in a way I had never heard her yell. The anger in her voice drained all the color out of my body.

She yanked Lizzy up by her hair and started pounding her tiny ribs with her hand. Lizzy cried out, screaming in octaves I had never heard in my life.

I panicked. Where was Master Sam? When would he get back from the factory? I made my way to the kitchen. It was still two hours until he would return.

Then I heard it.

CRACK.

The shrieks got higher.

Master Ally had broken my sweet Lizzy's bones. It was my fault. I had told her to be strong, kind, and good. I told her to shine kindness and this evil woman was dimming that light.

Rage overcame me and a thirst I did not realize I had been suppressing took over. I heard a roar and tasted blood. Soft flesh clamped between my strong jaws. I felt the crack of bones as if they were twigs under my feet in the jungle. For the first time, I let myself go and it felt so good. I fully surrendered to the animal they made me into.

"Lindy NO, NO, LINDY PLEASSSSEEEE!!" Lizzy's voice brought the room back into focus. I had my striped paw with my claws sunken into Master Ally's neck. Her warm blood trickled over them. Her face was an unrecognizable pile of blood, muscle, and skin, with her bones poking out in places. A part of me wanted to keep going. There was a wildness inside me I had never truly let loose.

I killed Master Ally.

It felt good.

I finally had control.

Then, as I looked over, I saw that Lizzy's eyes were full of terror and pain. I stood there, stunned. I tried to move but I could not I was in shock. Lizzy calmed her breath and looked at me, her eyes dim and hard. I could see her working out the situation. The reality that her mother was dead. Her mother was dead, and it was my fault.

I let myself turn back to my human form. The blood on my hands hit differently.

I murdered someone.

"They are going to kill you, Lindy. Get out." I looked at her, confused. Her eyes were full of something I had never seen. No one had ever looked at me that way. I saw the hate, but I also saw love. Lizzy loved me.

"GET OUT YOU STUPID HUMBLE AND DO NOT EVER COME BACK!" she shrieked as tears streamed down her face. She smacked my face getting blood on her hand. She looked at her mother's blood on her hand and sobbed even harder gasping. I wanted to scoop her into my arms, but I knew she was right. I could not stay here for both our sakes.

I turned around as the kitchen Humble opened the door. She looked me in the eyes with a slight smile. I paused to lock that slim delicate face into my memory.

"Lizzy, you have it in your heart to be good. Do not give in to them. Do not let their ignorant thoughts make you another dictator in a broken system. It is your choice. You can choose differently. You have the power to do so." I said this with a ferocity that I felt pulsing through my veins.

She stared at me in shock as tears streamed down her face. I morphed back into my animalistic self. I ran without knowing where I was going. I tested my tiger genes and felt the wind. I felt freedom, sadness, and regret pumping through my body.

I felt adrenaline.

When I finally stopped, I found myself looking at my reflection in the pool behind the continuation facility. I watched my reflection change, from an animal to my human form. My nose, mouth, frizzy hair, and my unchanging green eyes. I washed the blood off in the water. Then, without thinking, I stepped in.

A shot of white light went through my body as the ground began to sink beneath me. I was panicked but excited. I was escaping, but to what, I didn't know. That was when I collided with another part of myself.

That is when I met Lindsey, from Ella's world.

Chapter 17

Bert & Henry
~ *Ella* ~

I have always wanted to be able to read people's minds. The fact that Lindsey can read mine makes me very aware of my thoughts, in a way I have never been before. I can feel when she enters my brain. If only I could read hers.

I want to know why and how she escaped this world. Being in this factory and seeing Humbles slave away, I wonder what finally made her snap. *Did she know there were other dimensions? Or did she just run with hopes of something better?* I want to ask, and I feel I have every right to, since she can intrude into my thoughts at any time. Asking someone about their past is difficult. It is as if you are asking that person to undress in front of you. I know I should let her tell me in her own time.

Henry, however, has no issue asking me multiple questions about my past, trying his hardest to undress who I truly am. He never changes his facial expression, as if he is made of metal, and his voice is at the same even tone, constantly pronouncing anticlimactic judgements with each phrase.

"Were your parents very present, or were you mainly raised by a Humble?" He asks, looking straight ahead, as if this is a normal question. It is bold, due to the fact he is a Humble himself.

I start to answer when Bert jumps in with his friendly smile.

"Henry, that is impolite to ask when meeting Miss Ella." He smiles at me, as if he is trying to win me over. He is trying too hard. This baffles me, as I am eighteen, and these two men are at least twice my age.

This process continues, as Henry pounds personal questions from his stone mouth and clear, constant voice. Bert continues to bat them away with his jolly, bouncing ball phrases and antidotes. I ask questions that seem like something a boss would want to know, all the while trying to work on a possible escape plan.

Jack, of course, continues to follow. He keeps his eyes glued on the workers slaving away over computers, leather, and glue. Many of them make eye contact with him, as if they are welcoming him into the club. I am jealous of this connection. I am an instant assumed dictator.

Bert is kind and careful. He is a true people-pleaser, but I cannot tell how he would feel about betraying Elizabeth.

Henry is hard to read. He is monotone, direct, and there is a lot of underlying resentment. I hope that this ocean of lapping anger lying beneath his hard surface is enough to lead to movement.

We are in the crystal clean office, huddled around the computer, as Bert lays out the scheduling system. Henry is sitting in the corner, his eyelids heavy. I realize he has probably come in during the day just to meet me.

"Henry, you are welcome to go home. I know you will need to come in and take over in a couple hours. Is there a way I can reach you with any changes?" He looks up, surprised and relieved, the first facial expressions shown in the past three hours.

"Thank you, Miss Ella. Yes, your work device is in the top right drawer of your desk. The code is 061199. My contact is in there, under my name." He stays seated. I open the drawer and there is a slim piece of glass. I pick it up carefully and a blue light scans my face.

"Please enter the code," the piece of glass says in a robotic voice. Numbers appear and I press 061199 on the prompted keyboard. It then asks for my name. I enter Ella.

"It will now recognize your face, but remember the code, as it is what locks everything up. If you have any issues, feel free to ask me any time. I oversee security. You can view the multiple cameras throughout the building through your device. Bert and I can view this also, as it is how we keep an eye on the place 24/7. Any questions?" He is looking down as he delivers this casual information that I should understand.

"What if I forget the code? I am bad at remembering passwords." I say this trying to think of a way to lock him and Bert out of the system if it comes to that.

"I would suggest you remember it," he says, looking up.

"What do the numbers signify? Maybe that will help me remember," I say, hoping to gain insight.

"I created the code. It is my daughter's birthday." Henry says stone cold once again.

"Thank you, Henry. You may go home." He smiles a forced smile and exits through the door without another word. I picture his daughter dirty at home sitting in a pile of trash and I start to tear up. There has to be an alternative.

"Don't worry about Henry, he can be weird." Burt says smiling, as if my worry has seeped into the air.

"Thank you, Bert. Do you happen to have a map or layout of the factory? I just want to familiarize myself with the property."

"Of course, Miss Ella. I will get you anything you ask." He smiles big, as if he genuinely enjoys being told what to do. He exits the office to grab copies off a printer in the back room of the first floor. I sit and take in the office.

It is beautiful and it is all mine. I have never had an office before. Who knew I would be running a shoe factory? I wish I could tell my parents. I wish I could tell them everything. I want to rub it in their face that no matter where they travel to, I have gone further than they ever will. I have had to immerse myself in a culture in a way they never could. I smile, proud of my win against them. I turn to tell Jack of my accomplishment, but he is not behind me. He is not in the office at all. I get up suddenly, about to rush out and find him, as Bert enters the room, laughing, with Jack trailing behind him. Bert immediately shuts his mouth, stopping the laughter.

"I apologize, Miss Ella." He says looking at the ground. Jack is looking at me and winks. I feel my face turn pink, blushing.

"It is fine, Bert. Jack can be quite funny. Did you get the print outs?" I grimace feeling once again left out.

"Yes, of course, Miss Ella!" He hands them to me, and I catch him side-glance at Jack. He looks back at me quickly and I pretend to not have seen it. "I need to get back to work." He smiles and exits the room.

"I think it's time for us to go Miss Ella," Jack says beaming. I blush again and nod my head. I know he figured something out, but I am more excited that he is looking at me again. My heart is fluttering in happy heart beats. We get in the car and zoom back to the house. Jack bops his head back and forth as if he is listening to music the whole time.

When we arrive at our house and walk inside Jack turns to me.

"What?" I say, and he just smirks. "Jack come on tell me!"

"Ella, I got the floor plans! I got the floor plans of the underground tunnel system! Bert invited me over and printed them off for me. We are in!" He comes over and hugs me and it feels so good I want to cry. He lets go and starts walking around the kitchen. "This is great Ella! I can go over to his house and map out the escape. We can get out of this hell world soon. It's almost over!"

He is so happy, and I want to be too.

It is almost over.

I will go back to being nobody and alone. The burn and tingle rise in my nose once again.

"I am going to make sure the blinds are closed." I choke out the words.

"Why Miss Ella? You wanna give me a smooch?" He smirks once again oblivious to the fact I am almost in tears. I have never seen him so flirty and full of life. I manage a scoff and walk out to check the blinds. I hope he will follow me and take me into his arms and kiss me. As I walk away, my footsteps fill the high ceiling and I hear him open the fridge.

I want to ask him if he really thinks our choices here can influence our choices in the other dimensions like Steve said. *Do all our actions really influence the overall energy in the Universe?* If so, I do not know if I am actually helping. I want to talk about my mom. I want to talk about my middle name. I want him to hold me. Instead, I walk to my big fluffy bed and cry myself to sleep, wishing Lindsey would appear.

Chapter 18

Night with the Boys
JACK

Not falling for Ella has proved harder than I thought. I try to stop thinking about her as I walk towards the factory.

I am meeting up with Bert and some of the others from the factory for beer and poker. Some things aren't different across the dimensions, I guess. They were shocked when I told them my master wouldn't mind me hanging for a bit. I felt like a silly teenage boy bragging that mom is letting him go to the movies. Something I have never gotten to feel in real life. I never had a mom give enough shits where being allowed to do something was ever an issue.

This is one of the many factors that contributes to me being a slight alcoholic. Ella is another factor. Regardless, my mouth is watering for that beer.

I am so torn about Ella. I know she is better than the role she is playing. She is turning more and more heartless. Part of me hates her. I think of ways to kill her in her sleep. Smothering her with a pillow, poisoning her drink, or just hitting until she stops. Stops breathing. Stops demanding. Stops pitying herself for her 'hard' situation.

Then there is another part of myself that wants to wrap her in my arms and kiss her softly. A part of me that doesn't mind so much she is ordering me around. A part of me that is fine with all of it as long as she is at least near me. I love her. That's the part of me that I hate.

She is distracting me from who I want to be.

Sometimes I wish we could just be normal people. Go on a date. Have a first kiss that is just a lovely first kiss. Not a kiss that is laced with scheming, anger, and pain.

I know I am meeting up with Bert and his buddies to get intel, but I am excited to throw back and be free for a second. Be free from Ella.

Bert is standing at the shack in the back of the factory waiting for me. He greets me with a big hug and holds out a beer. I almost salivate.

"Ready to get started, my friend?", he says with a grin.

"Hell yeah, cheers!", I say, and he clinks his glass with mine. I take big glorious gulp and exhale. I follow him down the steps into the tunnel with a smile. Halfway down the stairs I start feeling dizzy. These beers must be way stronger than ours back home. I continue to follow him through the dark. It smells of piss and sewage. My head gets so full I feel lopsided. What the hell is in this beer? I fall sideways and a guy pushes me off and spits in my face.

"Bert, where are you?", I hear myself mumble. He comes up beside me and holds me up. His shirt is soaked through with sweat.

"It's okay buddy. I will get you there safe. You sure are a light weight." His voice is trembling.

Where is he taking me? The air around me constricts. *Sharon help. Please.* I plead in my head.

Calm down Jack you will be alright. They are on your side. I want to believe her but when does getting drugged ever mean the person is on your side? I start to panic. *Jack, please calm down. They are going to question you. Tell them the truth. You need them and they need you. Make sure they know that.* I start breathing in and out.

She is right. I am here for them. I am here to make things right. My vision starts to narrow in on a navy-blue women's shoe then everything goes black.

Chapter 19

Leather

~ *Ella* ~

Tonight is the night.

The night where Jack gets the intel and I sit alone. The night where all the power I have gained in this alternate world means nothing.

I always thought that after I found the other world I have been looking for since a child, I would never feel lonely again. I thought I would make plenty of friends and be the hero.

I am far from a hero.

I am more of a fake villain. I cannot believe he has just left me in the dust. We were supposed to do this together. We were supposed to be a team, not the Jack show.

I pour myself wine that I find in the small kitchen I have not entered since the first day we arrived. I start to run around the empty house, singing and dancing. I try to forget about both worlds I know. They are both lonely, boring, and do not have any magic. The most magical thing I have seen since this journey started is shoes appearing from machines in a factory. Worst magic trick ever.

I finish the last sip of the bottle, feeling the grit fall down my throat, when my doorbell rings. *Why would Jack ring the doorbell?* I slam the bottle down on the dining room table with a thud and tumble towards the door. I open it and, to my surprise, Elizabeth is standing in front of me with Ester trailing behind her, holding up Jack. He looks like he is whimpering and barely holding his head up.

"What happened?" I hear myself say. My heartbeat has taken over my body. I feel the thud of it in every crevice. I try my best to keep my worries behind the wall of my surgically altered face, but the wine has made it all loose.

"I spotted Jack walking on the street just a few moments ago at ten. I asked him what he was doing, and he crudely told me that he was visiting friends. When I asked him if he had your permission, he said he does not need your permission. He was obviously drunk and tried to run away from me. I ordered Ester to shoot a dart into his foot. This dart will kill off all the nerves in each toe, one by one, until they fall off. Now I know he is yours to punish, but I just could not let myself be treated like that. I hope you are not upset with me. I will not report this to the jury, as I have already overstepped enough."

My head starts to swim. *Darts. Jury. The woman with the bright eyes.* Then it clicks. *She is the woman in the dream where I end up in a pile of dead bodies.*

I feel my blood go cold.

She has essentially cut off one of Jack's toes. I wish the ground would sink beneath me like it did in the woods that night with Lindsey. Lindsey hears my panic. *'Ella, calm down. Tell her thank you and that you will surely punish him further. Explain that you gave him permission due to personal reasons.'* Lindsey sooths.

"Elizabeth, thank you so much for your diligence. I will certainly punish him further for these horrible words. I did give him permission to go to a friend for dinner, as I needed a night to myself. The drunken rudeness is inexcusable. I sincerely apologize." I hear myself say this and feel my face form the look of embarrassment.

She nods and tells me to not worry.

Ester pushes Jack's limp body onto mine without making eye contact. She then follows Elizabeth, not looking back.

I look at Jack and his eyes are full of tears. He lets out a gasp as we hobble over the door frame. His breath smells of beer and cigarettes. I help him hobble to the couch and fling him down a bit more aggressively than intended. He moans, motioning towards his foot.

I enter the kitchen for the third time since our arrival, frantically shoveling ice into a dish rag with my hand. When I get back to the couch in the dimly lit room, he has managed to roll up the leg of his jeans.

"Ella I don't know what happened. I am soooo sorry. It's all a blur. Ella please. Jack's shack. Shack Jack. Is whack." Jack drunkenly mumbles and then starts laughing an odd laugh in the back of his throat.

Tears stream out of his eyes and his laugh turns into a whimper.

"Give me your belt" I say. He does without question. I stick it in between his teeth. I have no idea what I am doing. I yank the dart out and he screams biting down on the leather. I start to untie his shoe and slowly shimmy it off his foot.

He is whimpering and shaking the entire time.

I then slowly peel the sock off and he starts to scream and move his body violently. The wine that was dancing through my body has completely vanished. With my sober eyes I realize his toe came off with the sock. Surprisingly, there is not a lot of blood. It is just gone, leaving red flesh pushing out of his skin.

I want to vomit.

I place the ice where his toe used to be. His squirmy body starts to come to ease. He pulls his hands out from under him. They are white from him squeezing the edge of the couch cushion.

I am lucky I was given the role of a Master. I feel guilty and wish I could make this all better. Jack takes the belt out of his mouth and examines his teeth marks in the leather, tracing them with his finger.

"Why did you put my belt in my mouth?" He asks quietly. He has seemed to sober up some but is still swaying back and forth.

"I do not know Jack. I must have seen it in a movie. I've never helped someone get through a toe amputation before." I say, short and annoyed. It is not his fault. I know I should not be mad at him but I am. If I went on the mission, I would not have gotten drunk and mouthed off at a Master. *Would've I?*

"I felt like a person Ella. For the first time since we have been here. I felt like a human being. I remembered what it is like to just live without being terrified every second. I was not scared. I was just shooting shit like I do with my buddies back home. It is what I do at home to escape, and I really needed an escape here. It's too much." He does not look at me and continues to trace his teeth marks on the belt.

I realize I have no idea what it is like for him here, or on our earth. He is always a Humble. He is always being submissive to someone, the Masters here are simply different. On this Earth, it is any person with brown hair, white skin, and blue eyes. At home, it is his alcoholic foster dad.

I leave the ice on his foot and sit beside him on the couch. I grab his hand that is tracing the marks back and forth and intertwine my fingers into his. I expect to feel the electricity that has been lingering in the air all along. I don't. I look up and he is looking straight into my eyes.

"I want to just feel like a person Ella." He whispers as our faces inch closer until our lips touch. It is warm, safe, and exciting all at the same time. Then it is nothing. The chaos underneath the surface is gone. The dark parts of him that connect us has vanished.

I pull back quickly, and he laughs in the back of his throat just as he did drunkenly a moment ago. The laugh still doesn't sound like him. He just doesn't laugh a lot and never like that. I lean my head on his shoulder trying to make it make sense. *What has changed?* I just can't shake the feeling something is off.

It's that laugh.

"I never thought my first kiss would be with someone who only has nine toes," I say, nudging him lightly. I want to hear the laugh again. I want to make these feelings make sense.

"Too soon Ella," he says laughing hard. The happy warm laughter rings through the air and my skin crawls.

It is not him.

It can't be. *What happened to him?*

I want to ask him. I want to slap him. Tell him to snap out of this facade. I want him to come back to me. I do not say anything and sit with his arm around me.

He looks like my Jack and sounds like my Jack. I am panicked and confused. I feel the weight of the dead bodies on my chest. I picture Elizabeth shooting a dart, winking. I truly hope that dream was a metaphor, but in the pit of my body I know it is not.

"Thank you, Ella. For everything," Jack interrupts my thoughts. I try to smile but can't. *Am I just telling myself it is not him to create distance?* I know that part of me hopes I that am not the one in the pile of dead bodies. It is such a selfish, dirty thought. Either way, this is not going to end well.

I can feel it.

Chapter 20

The Plan
~ *Ella* ~

Jack lays out the map of the underground tunnels on the table. He has already drawn out the escape route. He talks me through it. "Bert is on our side, but Henry is questionable. Bert himself has told me Henry is an extremely private person. Henry also admires Elizabeth with googly eyes every time she enters the room. Apparently, she did him a favor that he owes her for, forever. Whatever she did, she has him wrapped around her finger.

Bert knows where Henry lives in the trash pit. He has three daughters and one of them works at the factory. She is close with James, your mom's boyfriend. Bert is going to talk with James this week, to see if he and Lindy, Henry's daughter, can do a favor for him. We are going to make Henry believe that his oldest daughter has disappeared. This will make him late for work because he will frantically be searching for Lindy. This will allow us to exit the tunnel system with the AM and PM shifts.

You will lead the escape and will give a speech, making all the employees believe they are being punished for production numbers being down. You will say that we are taking a field trip, to teach them a lesson. That way, if we get stopped, we can continue this story and not risk exposure.

Bert and I will spread a rumor that you are taking us to the extermination center. Since that is the last above-ground building before we are out of Fernweh, the route will make complete sense. You are going to claim we are going through the underground tunnels to be an example to all other Humbles. How does that all sound to you?"

"Jack that's an amazing plan! It is genius. The only thing is, what if Henry passes us on his way to work? He will not believe me and will alert Elizabeth right away." I respond. This question hangs in the air. I am already thinking of a million more.

They all have daughters, sons, wives, and many more connections they will be leaving behind. Also, what about James? We cannot sacrifice James. I do not know if it is because of my middle name, the name of my gun, my 'moms' boyfriend, or maybe I am sometimes considerate, but we cannot leave him to stay behind. He will be taken in for questioning. He will be killed. *What about my mom, whom will she have now?*

"Good point. We will have to think of a more detailed plan for Henry. Maybe we can lead him to Lindy and tie him up somewhere." Jack brings me out of my rapid thoughts.

"Maybe I can get one of those dart guns from Elizabeth and say it is for you. I bet she has one that knocks people out. I had a dream about it." Jack is looking at me like I am insane.

"Ella, we cannot shoot someone with a dart. You have no idea how painful that is. Just because Henry and Elizabeth have some sort of understanding does not mean he should be thrown in with the dead bodies." I know he is right. I agree with him.

I do not want to be responsible for anyone's death.

"Do you want to get out of here alive with 200 people safe or not Jack? I think if we are going to sacrifice someone, it should be Henry, not James. They will want at least one body to put on trial and kill for the disappearance of 200 people" I respond, wishing I could stop the words coming out of my mouth. Jack is looking at me with disgust and nods. I just do not understand how I am the bad guy, when the sacrifice plan was his in the first place. In this world I always feel like the bad guy.

Maybe I am.

"Look, Bert knows each of these people better than we do. We need to listen to him. He says James is one of the most trustworthy guys and he would do anything to get your mom to safety. Bert said he will be willing to make the sacrifice. Ella, I am sure she will be ecstatic to be free. James will be protecting our mission by distracting Henry. He will be willing to do it and will not rat us out. I really do trust them both. I have a gut feeling."

I do not want to agree with him, but he has gotten to know them better than I have.

"What if we give James the mission to shoot Henry with the dart gun? Just to knock Henry out. We make him think it is from Elizabeth. That way, when James is questioned, he has a shot at surviving. Henry will come to and be reunited with his daughter and the blame will fall on Elizabeth not James."

"Okay, now we just need to carry this out on a day Elizabeth is terribly busy and will not have a reason to stop by. What about -".

"I'll meet with Elizabeth and figure out that part," I interrupt. I need to speak with her. Despite the fact she is horrible and shot off Jack's toe, I want to see her one last time. For some reason, part of me wants to tell her our plan. I will not, of course. *What if she is good? What if she is on our side?* I am most likely only having these thoughts because I want her to be. Also, Jack still seems off. I can't determine if it's me or him.

I just want to be away from him.

Chapter 21

My Arrival
[Lindsey]

As the ground sank beneath me, I barely felt my first sliding. That bright white light walked me through the life of Lindsey.

Not me, but the Lindsey I was about to meet. I saw her abandoned by her husband. I saw her raising her son on her own. I saw her son getting happily married. I felt her jealousy of the love her son had for his wife. I felt the resentment she felt towards her son and his father. All the sacrifices she made for both and in the end they both threw her aside for some bright blue-eyed idiot who probably could not even use a hammer. I felt her sadness when her son's wife came asking for money because her son developed a drinking problem. They were living off his wife's waitressing money.

The rage that was pulsing through my veins as I tasted Ally's blood returned when the wife came home to tell Lindsey she did what was best for her son. In her eyes, what was best included adding arsenic to his most recent drink. I felt the rage as seventy-year-old Lindsey reached out and strangled the beautiful dainty girl in all pink. I feel the sadness as Lindsey realizes what she has done. The shock. The same shock I felt when I looked down at the pulpy remnants of Master Ally's face. However, this Lindsey and I are different in one way.

I had dreamed of doing what I did to Master Ally for years. I know it is wrong, but I liked the taste of her blood. I liked letting myself go.

I liked winning for once.

This Lindsey I was about to meet had not dreamed of this moment with her daughter in law. It was a moment of rage she did not know she was capable of. She viewed it as a loss, a huge loss, and had decided it was her last one.

All these emotions and events flashed through my mind as I slide into Ella's world. I arrived with a thump in Ella's closet to find the woman who had just shared her story with me hanging from the ceiling. The stench of stale smoke and old beets filled the closet. I had no idea where I was or what just happened.

I did what any rational person would do: I cried.

I cried for hours, long and hard.

I cried in a way I did not know I was capable of.

I cried with anger, sadness, and confusion.

Eventually, I stopped crying and pushed past my counterpart. Only to find that beautiful slim girl that I just saw strangled in my mind stuffed into a wooden box at the end of the bed on top of stuffed animals. She, for some reason, reminded me of a younger Master Ally, which made me shudder. I walked out of the room, down a long hallway with a wooden floor. The house was so small compared to the glamourous house I had been living in.

Then I heard a knock on the door.

"Lindsey are ya home? It's me Bob, I came over to check on you and read you our weekly book. This week I picked a sci-fi novel, but there is a love story. I really think you will like it." He stopped talking, so I crept into the back room and hid under the bed.

I wanted him to come in.

I wanted answers.

I also did not want to be stuck with two dead bodies. *'Come in'* I thought.

'Why yes I will' I felt him respond in his head. This was the first time I tapped into someone's mind. I have been able to do this ever since Lindsey killed herself and tapped me into hers. She opened my mind to the people of her world.

I lead him to the back of the hall, where he gasped and dropped his nerdy book. This is how I first met Bob.

Over the next week, I hung around the house as the police came in and out. I hid in closets and under beds. I also hid among the trees outside of the house. My catlike prowess helped me sneak around that house for years. The bodies got wheeled away and soon the house was empty.

Bob had a girlfriend, Wendy. I liked her. She was spunky and wore interesting clothes. They came around the house a lot. Bob really took the suicide hard, and Wendy was there to comfort him. They had good hearts. They were just a little too young and naïve.

After much observation, I decided I could put up with them and with my newfound power, I convinced them to buy the house. That same year they got married. Nine months later they had Ella.

While there is definitely love there, I did have a huge part in pushing them along. I needed a companion. Also, a huge part of me mourned Lizzy. I had lost her and had no idea how to get back to her. I wanted a daughter to call my own.

When they first brought Ella home, she was calm and looked around with big grey blue eyes. She was taking everything in.

She has always been curious and has always been completely fine being alone, even if she thinks she is not. Bob and Wendy had no idea I was lurking throughout their house every night.

They have never known.

During the day I would hunt in the woods behind the house. I would eat squirrels, rabbits, and, occasionally, a deer. I would feel guilty with bigger animals because I could never eat all the meat. At night, I would watch my darling baby girl sleep.

My Ella.

Those first four years were complete bliss. I got to hunt during the day and exercise my inner animal instincts: the instincts I awakened with my first kill. There was such a thrill to hunting. I never reverted to my tiger form, for fear I would be stuck that way. Hunting was still a breeze. I would tell the animal where to go and bring them right to me. I would sometimes toy with them a little bit before crushing them between my pointy teeth.

Then, after I was tired out, I would sneak back into the house and watch Ella play and grow. She has always been so smart. However, Bob and Wendy were getting too close. They wanted to take her on trips. They want to be around her all the time. They started to breach on Ella and my relationship.

Elizabeth had already been taken away from me by Fernweh and its systems. Part of me knew that one day I would come back and find Elizabeth ordering a Humble around. I would come back to see that all of my sacrifices paid off in no way. I, like the Lindsey hanging from the rope, made sacrifices and might never get the payback I deserve. With Ella, things were going to be different.

Ella is mine.

Wendy had her fashion line and it started to blow up. This led to a trip to Paris. They took Ella with them. It made me furious. I did not want to be separated from her again.

Using my powers, I made sure Ella was left behind for every trip going forward. I know it is wrong. I know I have truly isolated her from her family. I am her *true* family. Without me telling Bob and Wendy what to do, she would not exist.

I would do anything for my Ella. I know it really hurt her when I chased all those silly little girls away. They honestly were already judging her and putting her down in their minds. Why would I let her be surrounded by people like that? They were going to eventually let her down in some way or another. Like Amanda did. Amanda decided to neglect my Ella completely on her own. What kind of protector would I be if I just let people continue to treat her that way?

I do not regret nudging these people out of Ella's life. Because of my protection, Ella values herself even more than this boy she has fallen for. She tells herself she is not sure, but I know when it comes down to it, she will pick herself. Which in my opinion, based on what I have seen from the many minds I have entered, is something quite special to behold. I am so proud of her.

In case Ella does have a moment of weakness, Elizabeth is going to give what she owes. I am going to make sure Elizabeth saves my Ella. That is all I can thank her for. She has fallen into the same system as her mother upheld so strongly. Yes, Elizabeth is kinder and yes, has better opinions. However, she has not changed anything, other than preventing creatures like me from being made. Her own daughter is growing up in trash and she just stays silent. She disgusts me in a way I never thought possible.

I know this is not fair.

Motherhood makes us make decisions we are not always proud of. I just thought she was stronger. I hoped she would choose to be stronger. Ella will be stronger, and Ella will create change. That is where Steve and the organization comes in. Like I said everything was pure bliss with Ella and I the first four years.

Ella like me, had her fate decided for her on her fifth birthday.

Chapter 22

Hot Water

~ *Ella* ~

I raise the ring hanging out of the tiger's mouth and let it drop three times. I can feel my heartbeat pulsate throughout my body. I know she is not my friend but lying to her feels like betrayal.

Finally, Elizabeth comes to the door. She swings it open with gusto and her perfect hair, frizzed around the top of her head, gives her a Statue of Liberty look. Her sparkling eyes are more ignited than I have ever seen them before. Ester is not trailing behind her per usual. She seems to be alone.

"Good afternoon, Elizabeth. How are you?" I say. She squints her eyes into narrow rectangles. For a second, I wonder if she has forgotten who I am.

"Thank God it is you, I need a friend right now." Her voice is tired and hoarse. This is not what I was expecting. "Would you like some tea?" She quickly pulls me in and slams the door behind her. She runs to the kitchen, looking back over her shoulder.

"Is someone else here Elizabeth? Are you alright?" I ask.

"No, not yet." She brings me a cup of boiling water with a lemon slice in it. She completely forgot the tea bag. "Ella, enjoy your tea. I will be back down in a second." She runs up the velvet stairs, which is quite comical. She has always floated into rooms, not bobbed and bumbled around.

Holding my cup of hot water, I wander over to the bottom of the stairway. I stare into the tiger's eyes hanging over the woman's shoulders. That painting has always made my spine prick up.

Due to my impatience and nervousness, I am about to turn around and walk back home when the doorbell rings.

"Coming!!" Elizabeth yells. She shows up at the top of the stairs in a pleated blue dress, looking perfect and beautiful. I have no idea how she bounced back to her normal self so quickly. She glides down the stairs. Once she reaches the bottom, her sparkling blue's peer into a part of me that is deep and hidden. We are on the same page. I do not know what about, but we just are. She smiles a smile full of anxiousness and excitement.

The door swings open, and we are greeted by four men. They are all white, bald, and wearing circle shade sunglasses. They are huge and I know right away that whatever Elizabeth has done they are not too happy with it.

"Welcome to my home gentlemen", she beams a radiant smile. "This is my dear friend Ella. We have been chatting and having our afternoon tea, as usual. Is there something we can help you with?"

The man in the front of the pack glances at me up and down. His eyes end on my cup of hot lemon water. "Ma'am we have a search warrant for your home. It is just protocol, Miss Elizabeth. We know you are a very upstanding citizen and appreciate all you do for the board of continuation." The lead man pushes into the house, followed by the three men who look exactly like him. They pass us and head up the velvet staircase.

Elizabeth stays frozen in a smiling stupor. She looks like a porcelain doll. I am waiting for her to crack and crumble to the floor. She does not.

"Let's go to the kitchen and make more tea," she says. I follow.

"Who are those guys, Elizabeth?" I whisper. She turns and looks at me, still smiling. Her eyes are full of terror and on the verge of tears. She opens her mouth to speak, but it shakes as she is unable to get the words out. Giving up, she shuts it promptly and stares straight ahead.

I take my mug and sit at the table. She joins me and we sit in silence, listening to the four men stomp around above us. Their footsteps seem to trample above for hours. With each rip of a pillow, slam of a door, and crash of glass my heart continues to beat faster and faster. I am waiting for it to leap out of my chest. Finally, the four gentlemen descend the stairs.

"You are all clear, Miss Elizabeth. We apologize for the disturbance." The leader of the four shark-like men leaves with his fellow giants following him. As soon as the door slams Elizabeth lets out a gasp and her body starts shaking violently.

"Elizabeth, lets lay down okay?" I lead her over the couch across the foyer and cover her with a blanket made of a tiger's hide.

"Get. That. Off. Me." She says through gritted teeth. I carefully remove the hide and grab her a glass of water. She sits up slowly and drinks in dramatic gulps. Her heaving chest slows down, and color starts to return to her cheeks.

She looks up at me with a smirk.

"Ella, do you want to know a secret?" She laughs a throaty laugh that ripples under my skin.

Then she tells me about her family.

"Ester was my main caretaker and was left in charge of the Factory, along with my mother's friend, Veronica, after my parents' incident. So as a result, Ester mainly ran the factory, while Veronica occasionally popped her head into Ester and my life to play mother or boss. Then she would disappear back into her own life.

Henry, who you met the other day and runs the factory with Bert, always hid in the Humbles' shed while his mother came to work. She was constantly worried that he would be taken by the Agency for the continuation facility, so she kept him with her always. This does not happen often only if there is a shortage in babies for a season. But she was and still is a good and protective mother. She just doesn't like me very much." Elizabeth looks down at her hands and takes a deep breath.

"Anyway, I would get bored and wander around to explore while Ester checked on things at the factory. One day, I found Henry in the shed, trying to catch a mouse. I was lonely and was excited to have a friend, even if he was a Humble. After that, we regularly went on adventures together." She laughs in the back of her throat reminiscing. She clears her throat again and continues.

"As I got older, Veronica started to appear more often. Ester is a rule follower and taught me a lot, so I always knew exactly how to act and what to say. It was a lie. An act. I only felt free when I got to escape with Henry.

As we grew up, Henry started working at the factory and I moved into the role of managing it. We would sneak off together in the jungle and our friendship started to grow into something more. One day, after work, I disguised myself as a Humble and went home with Henry. He had a little shack made out of cardboard surround by trash, but I didn't care. We were in love. Ester came searching for me and she was furious."

Elizabeth pauses again.

This is a story that she has probably never told out loud.

"I still remember the day when I found out I was pregnant. I never get sick. Ester took me to the doctor, and it felt like it could not be happening to me. I did not know what to do. Ester scheduled an appointment for the baby to be secretly removed. I just could not do it. I could not kill Henry and I's child. I wanted to run away with him and raise the child together. Ester said the agency would come after us and we would both be killed in jury along with the child. That it was way too risky.

I arranged a secret meeting with Henry. He wanted to run away together too. I told him it would be best for me to just get rid of the baby. He begged me not to kill our child. He wanted to be a father. I was 16 and terrified, but I love that man with all my heart. So, we agreed he would take the baby and claim the mother died in childbirth. I just had one request. That he name her Lindy. I stayed cooped up in the house for nine months. From then on, I was home schooled. Ester did not want to risk anyone finding out. I have spent most of my life alone, besides Ester, board meetings, and visiting the factory. I have been alone for my daughter, Lindy, to have a life, even if it's not a great one."

As Elizabeth ends this story, she presses her lips into a hard line. "I have never told anyone this, Ella. She is my baby, Lindy. Giving her up to him was the hardest thing I have ever had to do."

She pauses and tears come to her eyes.

"Honestly, I do not think I would have been a good mother, anyhow, since my true mother left me too young. Now the Agency is snooping around my life. I am terrified they will find out and hurt my baby girl." I reach over and place my hand on hers.

"How old is your daughter?" I ask.

"Her birthday is June 11, 1999. So, that makes her 12? Wow, it is horrible I do not even know my own child's age." She responds. Then it clicks.

061199 is the code to the factory. The security cameras. Henry found out about our plan. Jack met Bert at the factory. Henry is protecting his family and the mother to his child.

"Why are they investigating you?", I ask.

"Well, they have been alerted that someone within the factory is planning an escape. So, naturally, they are investigating me as the owner." She replies.

"You know, I never understood why she stood up for me. Why she risked her life for me. Why my true mother sacrificed her sanity for me? Now I know. I will do anything to make sure my daughter is safe." She stares at me, and we do have an understanding.

She knows.

She knows that Lindy and Henry are the scapegoats for our plan.

"I should get going Elizabeth, are you sure you will be okay?" I say smiling.

"Yes of course! I would go check on Jack if I were you. I've always loved boys night, you find out so much" She goes to the kitchen avoiding eye contact with me.

Boy's night? Bert must have told her. Jack and the plans of the underground tunnel! I abruptly get up and run out the door.

Part of me knows I need to calm down. Part of me questions what the hell was I thinking, trusting her? Most of me just cares about Jack. I arrive to our door and make myself stop. *Lindsey, I kind of need your help here* I think impatiently. *'I am here Ella. Keep yourself composed.'* Lindsey replies.

I enter, making myself smile, to find Jack handcuffed at the bottom of the stairs. There is anger radiating from his body. He shoots a look at me that says, 'where the hell have you been'?

"Excuse me!!" I call out. The thundering footsteps move together until the four big men arrive at the top of the stairs. As they descend, one of them is holding papers.

My heart drops. I keep my face plump and alive, as if those papers are not the end of me.

"Ma'am, do you know what these are?" The leader says, as he shoves the papers towards me. I grab them carefully conveying a look of confusion on my face.

"It seems to be some sort of map" I reply.

"Yes, it is of the underground system." He booms. His eyes are dissecting my thoughts. I can feel the words start to form in my mouth. *'Do not say a word, Ella'* Lindsey's voice coos.

"Why would I have a map of the underground system. I do not want be around all of *them*." I scoff at his ridiculous implication.

"Ma'am, we believe your Humble is planning to escape. We are going to take him in to a holding cell for the night. His interrogation will take place tomorrow at noon. You are required by the Agency board to be present. You might also be interrogated yourself if evidence suggests your involvement." The words echo through my brain. I cannot form a response.

I am in shock. I take a deep breath in.

"Thank you for your time. May I have a moment with my Humble before you take him?" Lindsey guides me in this reply. It comes out of my mouth spewing anger, and I glare at Jack. The four men exit and close the front door behind them waiting outside. I stay frozen in place.

"Jack, I am so sorry. I don't know what to do."

"Ella, you have done enough. Did you go and tell your bff Elizabeth? I saw them come from her house" Jack spits.

I am completely blindsided. Jack thinks I would sell him out? "Jack I had no idea. I do not even know who these men are! Everything is so complicated. Henry is trying to protect his family. You have to believe me. It's me Ella. Please?" I look into his golden eyes for confirmation we are good.

They are not golden anymore.

"Whatever you say Master. Don't even bother showing up tomorrow. I am already dead. We both know that." He glares at me his golden-brown eyes dark as wet slate. "This was the plan all along, huh? You and Elizabeth throw me under the bus so you can run off with lover boy? Huh? ANSWER ME!!" He yells through gritted teeth. I am so confused. *What is he talking about?* Before I can ask, the four bald men swing open the door.

"Miss Ella, we are taking your Humble now. You will be under surveillance until the interrogation tomorrow. Do not even think about leaving this house. Do you understand?" I nod in agreement and the huge men heave Jack up and carry him out, slamming the door behind them.

I sink to the ground in shock.

Jack thinks I betrayed him. Also, *what was he talking about?* My head hurts. I know I should dissect what he yelled at me. Maybe it is a clue. *Is there any point?* I failed him and the mission.

Chapter 23

Rabbit in a cage
JACK

Nothing is going how it is supposed to.

Nothing is how it seems.

Sharon is nowhere to be found. She won't answer me. She is supposed to be there for me but once again I am alone. Everyone always leaves me. I thought Ella was the one in the dark here, but it has been me all along.

When I came to after tumbling behind Bert, a musty basement floor came into focus. My feet and hands were tied, and I was strapped to a chair. Then I saw the navy-blue women's shoes. For a moment, I panicked thinking it was Ella, but as my eyes traveled up to meet hers, my panic turned to terror.

Miss Elizabeth has many sides. She always seems so stuck up and prompt but there she sat legs uncrossed, leaning back, drinking a beer.

"I hear you like our beer here Jack….." She said my name as if it was a new word to her, metallic running around her mouth. I was about to spit in her face, then I saw him.

Jack from Perfect Earth.

"Hey bud, don't do anything stupid alright?", he said through gritted teeth. I was about to yell and call him a traitor when I realized he was tied up too.

"What do you want?" I spat out evenly glaring at Elizabeth.

"Jack, don't be upset. I am smarter than I look, what can I say? I recognized you the moment I saw you with sweet Ella. At first, I thought, what is Jack up to now. Then we got to hang out a couple times and I paid attention. While you are the spitting image of the crook, thief, and lowlife Jack that I know, you are smarter. Unfortunately, not smarter than me.

So, I went and found the Jack I know in his shack full of sham goods that he sells taking advantage of poor people. Do not worry. He filled me in. I know you are here to light the courthouse on fire with everyone in it.

How could you do that to Ella? You know her and I are becoming friends and she really cares about you. How could you do that to my friend Jack and Jack?", Elizabeth's lips turn into a mocking smile.

I feel my face go white. How am I always the one getting screwed?

"Don't worry boys, I am not mad. I really like the idea. The only thing is, I don't want to be in the room when it burns. Burning alive is a rough death. I think we can all agree." she pauses looking back and forth between Jack and I. He is looking at the floor. She keeps going.

"So, here's the new plan boys. We will still burn the courthouse down. However, I am not so sure you will both live. If either of you. I really debated who to sacrifice." She looks over to Jack from Jack's shack.

"Jack you and I have history, don't we? I have really wanted to pay you back for what you stole from me. You will go back to Ella tonight and tomorrow you will be taken to the courthouse. I will personally ensure you do not leave that building alive. Understood?" Jack nodded still looking at the floor.

"You on the other hand, I do not particularly hate. I haven't decided how to use you yet. Bert will keep you locked down here until I decide. Do you have preferences you would like to share regarding your stay?" Elizabeth asked me smirking.

"Just let me burn it down. Please. I just want to watch it burn." I look at her right in the eyes as I mumble my request. Surprise hits her face quickly then it bounces back to mockery. Jack of perfect earth is glaring at me.

"What a sweet Jack. I will try to accommodate.", Elizabeth shrugged then stood up as Bert handed her a gun. She turned around and shot a dart into Jack from Jack's Shack foot. He whimpered as Bert opened his throat and poured a liquid down it. Elizabeth walked over to me gun still in hand. I started to squirm then everything faded away once again.

. . . .

I came to in this disgusting, stinking jail cell. I think over and over what I did wrong. I keep yelling and yelling out to Sharon. *Where the hell is she?* This is why you shouldn't trust the devil. I yell her name in my head and sometimes out loud. Bars surround me on all sides. As I yell, I start to bang my head against the bars.

I need out.

I just want out.

My mind drifts as I continue to scream and bang my head.

I remember the soft green grass. I was crouching at the edge of the woods when it hopped out. A baby rabbit. I wanted a pet so badly.

My foster parents told me no pets were allowed. I accepted this until I found a cage by the dumpster, and I knew it was fate. He just hopped right into my trap. His fur a mix of black, brown, and grey with a white belly underneath. I petted him and held him to my chest. He didn't bite and seemed happy. I put him back in the cage and carried him home and went straight to my room.

As the day went on, he got anxious. He was wild and not used to the cage. He started banging his head against the side. I would take him out, hold him to my chest, and his heartbeat would lower. Then, I would place him back in the cage.

We went through this about 7 times and I got fed up. He just needed to learn how to be in the cage. I went down to help make dinner. My host parents and I watched a movie.

I liked them; they were nice. After the movie, I snuck some carrots out of the fridge to take to my new fury friend. When I opened my door, the cage had moved halfway across the room and there was a trail of blood. He had smashed his head again and again on the edge of the cage until his head split. I could see the bone poking out through the meaty pulp of a gash. I dropped the carrots in the puddle of blood and knelt.

He was still breathing and slightly whimpering. I opened the cage and put my hand around his tiny neck.

I twisted quickly.

CRACK.

I feel my nose break as I come back to my own jail. Pain shoots up through my skull. I have banged my head so hard against the bars, I have broken my nose. I touch my nose and feel it being sideways. My vision starts to grey out.

I am not meant to be caged.

I am wild too.

I don't have Sharon to whisper a lullaby, so I whisper my own.

"Red hands.

Red tears.

Smear it around to know you're still here.

Plucked Strings.

Hallow bones.

Red is the color of the tone."

- Jacks nightly lullaby.

Chapter 24

The Interrogation
~ *Ella* ~

Elizabeth shows up the next morning at ten. Her knocks wake me up. I fell asleep at the base of the stairs.

I open my eyes, slowly and confused. They are crusted together from dried tears. My throat is lumped up and I try to say 'I'm coming', but just a croak escapes.

As I sit up, it feels as if I am carrying a whole ocean in my head. My face is covered in dried salt from tears. I spent the whole night sobbing, with Lindsey occasionally soothing me. I do not like having someone in my head but having her there to share my broken heart and fear was comforting.

As I stand up, the first coherent thought that enters my head is *'Jack is going to be killed today'*. I am about to crumble back to the hard-cold floor when Elizabeth impatiently rushes in. She catches me and smiles. She must have known they were coming to my house next. *Why wouldn't she warn me?* I want to hit her. I want to scream at her. I want to tell her this is all her fault.

Instead, I lay my head on her shoulder. She leads me over to the couch.

"Why are you here?" I manage to let out.

"Because I had to go into an interrogation alone, and I lied to protect myself. I have had to do it all alone. And I wish someone were there to pick out my outfit and tell me I have nothing to worry about. Besides, it is not your fault the person you love was scheming behind your back. I could not imagine Henry betraying me like that." She stares at me.

I cannot tell if she knows or is refusing to accept the truth. I want to tell her everything. I want to explain that it was to help people escape. But how could she ever understand that I am here to help people escape her. To escape me. To escape the oppressive reality of their lives under the shoes of us: the rich. She could never possibly understand. To be honest, I do not even understand.

Now that I am faced with the consequences, I mourn for Jack, but I also hate him. The way he looked at me. The way he decided to leave things between us. If I die today, I deserve it but so does he. I have a strong feeling that I will not be that lucky. I have become so good at lying and saving myself first, every day, that it is the same as blinking. I will mourn Jack forever regardless.

I do not want it to end on this note.

I do not want it to end with him hating me and me hating him.

Where is my decision in this?

Elizabeth picks out a navy-blue suit with white pinstripes for me. She leaves at eleven since she is part of the judges' table. This surprises me, since it seems like a conflict of interest, but I am relieved. She seems to be on my side.

I arrive to a red brick building with white pillars. They pat me down as I enter. I go to the information desk and give my name and they direct me to court room 5B. I am escorted in and brought up to a stainless-steel cube besides the judge.

All the seats are arranged like a small Colosseum and in the middle is a stainless-steel floor with multiple metal loops. The audience is already half full and people stare as I take the steel throne. It smells like metal, sweat, and is thinly veiled with lavender cleaning products.

People continue to trickle in. I watch them, all white, brown hair, blue eyes in their blue clothing.

I hate them.

I feel my jaw protrude as they continue to enter. All the same. All looking like me.

The judges finally file in. There are eight of them. Elizabeth is the third to enter and the only female among them. Then the four big shark-like men enter the steel floor, dragging Jack between them. I almost break and let out a cry when I see him. Then I grit my teeth together. I love him and despite everything I still do. That will never change.

His eyes are black and blue bulges. His legs are covered in bloody lines. He is laying limp between the four men, like a dirty raggedy Ann doll. They lower him to the ground and connect his cuffs to two of the loops on the metal floor. I want him to look up at me. He does not. *Is he is already gone?*

"Let's get started!" Says the one of the judges next to Elizabeth. "Bring out our first witness." The big men bring out James, from the factory, and chain him up besides Jack. They have a microphone in front of him. I cannot believe they chain their witnesses to the floor. I immediately understand that these witnesses, the Humbles, are already considered guilty. No matter what James says, he will be found guilty. I was naïve to think that any Humble left behind involved in our plan would live. I wonder if he will choose the truth or to lie. I wonder what I would do if I knew in the end it does not matter.

"James, did you know of Jack's escape plan?"

"No, your honor. I was not aware of the plan until his arrest," he mumbles staring at the ground. I swallow hard trying to keep composure. Jack looks over at him abruptly.

He's alive.

"She had everything to do with this. This is her fault." Jack whispers into the mic in front of him. My heart beats a little out of my chest. *Is he referring to me?*

"You only speak when you are spoken to!" The old bald judge yells. One of the shark men crosses over and back hands Jack hard, leaving his head to lay limp once again. He does not let out a whimper. I want to yell at everyone to stop.

I want to cry.

I feel my lip quiver.

I also feel Elizabeth glaring at me.

"How did you find out about this plan, James?" The judge asks.

"Jack had told Bert, our manager, that he wanted to take everyone from the factory to help us all escape. But they did not want to take everybody. They wanted me to stay behind. They wanted me to take Henry's daughter hostage, so he would come looking for her. They did not want Henry or I to go with them. I do not know why." I can feel Elizabeth gasp. I can feel her anger from across the room. It sounds so bad now that I know what I know. It sounds so bad out loud.

"Jack what do you have to say to this?" The judge booms. Half unconscious he responds.

"Jack did it, not me.", He mumbles barely able to lift his head and it breaks my heart. He is talking nonsense.

The crowd lightly laughs as his response. I feel the rage underneath the surface boiling over. I feel the churning of what I have marked as sadness, loneliness, helplessness bubble up. Those were just polite words for my manic feelings of anger.

"What do you mean, you are not Jack?" The judge asks with a smirk. The crowd laughs lightly once again.

"The other Jack did it. Not me. It is her fault too." Jack responds. He looks up at me and glares. He is not making any sense. *What other Jack? How hard did they hit him? Why would he bring me down with him?*

Part of me understands his anger. I have been so cruel ordering him around. Taking out my stress on him. At the same time, he has disregarded me. He went on with his plan without consulting me and look where it got us. *Why didn't he just open up to me? Why didn't he include me? Did he think I can't handle it?* That doesn't sound like my Jack. We both know we can handle a lot. I look long and hard at the man chained to the metal floor. I think of that laugh. The kiss we exchanged that was empty. Maybe he is not out of it after all.

Could it be possible?

"Ella, is this true regarding your involvement?" The judge looks over at me in my steel box. *Lindsey, I need you. Lindsey where are you? Lindsey please!* She enters my brain I can feel her presence, but something is wrong. She is not calm. She is panicked. *'Tell Elizabeth she gets to choose. The little pond of water is the escape. Behind the continuation facility.'* Then she is gone.

Something is wrong with Lindsey. All I know is she wants me to escape. I take a deep breath in and one out. My breath echoes in the microphone in front of me throughout the colosseum.

I look at Jack's bloody body.

"Your honor, I had no knowledge of this plan. This Humble is obviously out of it. He doesn't even know his own name." It is as if I am watching myself say this with a mocking smirk.

So cruel.

This is not me. This cannot be me. I would not summon someone to death to save myself. But it is me and I am.

I am choosing me.

"So, you are saying, a Humble, came up with this grand plan all by themselves? With no education, no prior learning of maps, came up with a plan to steal 200 people?" The main judge says. The patronizing tone, and the steal 200 people as if they are his personal property.

"I think that Jack and any Humble is capable of that and a lot more your honor. Not to be rude, but you should really be careful of how much you are underestimating these people." I say. The crowd holds their breath. You can feel the silence. The judge is at a loss for words. His already blotchy red face grows darker in shade. He is about to rebuttal when Elizabeth interrupts.

"Your honor I think I understand where Ella's rude comment stems from. Jack, how long have you had relations with Ella?" Elizabeth asks in her cool voice. I know she is mad about her daughter. I know she knows I was involved. The crowd gasps, including me. I do not look in her direction.

'Jack' is completely thrown off.

"It did not mean anything. I just do what my Master says." His brown eyes are looking into mine. This can't be my Jack. It isn't. My Jack knows we are so much more. We always have been for each other. *Why would he deny that?* I want to scream and yell, but I know us both being dead will not do any good. Lindsey is in trouble, I could feel it.

"That will be all." I hear the judge say in the background. He motions his hand and two of the giant guards come out with guns.

One is pointed at James; one is pointed at Jack.

"On this day, James is sentenced to death for attempted kidnapping and assisting with a terrorist operation. On this day, Jack is sentenced to death for running a terrorist operation and for inappropriate relations with a master." The crowd starts cheering. My broken and angry heart is their entertainment. If there is the slightest chance this is my Jack, shouldn't I stop this? Shouldn't I try to?

James starts screaming "I did not know! This is not my fault!" He is spewing and glaring at me, saliva escaping his mouth with each word. All I can think of is my poor mother. She will cry when she hears the news. Jack is not even looking at me. He is starting at the metal floor. Whether he is my Jack or not he is part of Jack. He is a version of Jack.

These are people and their lives.

"STOOPPPP!" I scream so loud and thundering I surprise myself. I am standing on the seat in my steel throne holding the mic in my hand. The whole coliseum is dead quiet. All eyes on me.

"What is wrong with you people? Yes, Jack made the plan. He made the plan because he is smart and clever. James is right. This is not his fault. James is a good man and makes my mother happy in a way I have never seen her. So please do not kill them. Please have mercy. Let us go. We will all disappear and never come back." The silence hangs in the air. Elizabeth is looking at me with a mixture of shock and awe. She almost looks.......proud?

"Thank you, Ella." The judge clears his throat and motions for the two guards to continue. The shots ring out in the air and the crowd cheers.

I go numb.

It feels as if a fog comes over everything. *What have I done? What was I thinking?*

They drag Jack's and James bodies out of the coliseum. Both limp, with blood flowing from their heads. Jack's eyes are on me but there is nothing left in them. Cleaning staff rushes out, wiping up the blood. Lavender hits my nose. I half expect to wake up in my bed on the house on the hill, but nothing happens. This is not a dream or even a nightmare.

Two of the large guards come grab my arms and lift me out of the steel box and throw me on the cold metal floor. My arms are chained to the loops. The ground is still damp from the blood that was just wiped away.

"On this day, Ella is sentenced to death for relations with a Humble, being a descendant of a Humble, and having knowledge of a terrorist operation. Any last words Ella?" The microphone is plopped down in front of me, and I can hear my breath come in and out. The silence is once again in the air with all eyes on me. I look up at Elizabeth who is now looking at me with a stone face. *Did I imagine her reaction before?*

I think of Lindsey's words. "You have a choice, Elizabeth. You have the power to have one." I say and her eyes widen.

She looks as if she was struck by lightning.

"Thank you, Ella. These rules are in place for a reason. Your kind will never understand." The judge replies. He motions for the guards to bring out a gun.

"Wait!" Elizabeth yells. "This disgusting Humble claimed to be my friend. I gave my factory to her in confidence, and this is how she has repaid me. By trying to steal my workers. If it is okay with you, I would like to do the honors myself." She says these words viciously and I can feel the fire pulsing through her veins.

The judge nods approval and she walks down the stairs from the judges' table. She goes into the back room and comes out with a gun in her hand. She aims it at me as the crowd starts to cheer once again. She puts her hand on the trigger and winks at me as she pulls it. Just like my dream.

Except this isn't a dream.

Everything fades to black.

Chapter 25

Jack's Shack
JACK

I am woken up by a bright white light shooting through my body. Then I see Jack from Jack's shack. He is a young boy. He sees Elizabeth climbing over trash with another boy. He runs over and asks if he can play. She laughs cruelly and says no and tells him to get lost. He runs to the bottom of the volcano and cries.

Then as if I am watching a slide show on old film, my view flicks forward.

He steals books from the Master's library and is reading about cross dimensional traveling. He starts building his shack. Every piece built with a trade. A book for some wood. Medicine (leaves he mashes up and adds water to) for nails. He also collects metal.

Much like the capsule Ella and I stepped into to travel here from the In Between, he builds one in the back of the shack. Jack has a lot of test runs that did not go too well. At one point he was suspended in a limbo space of just black for what seems like years. That didn't stop him, he got the kinks worked out.

He travels to another dimension and meets another Jack. He is filled with excitement. Then the door opens. The man is older in his 50's.

"You here for a girl?", the man says. In the background women are chained to the walls. They are swaying slowly in different directions unable to hold up their heads.

"Uh no I am looking for Jack", Jack from Jack's shack says.

"That's me, come on in!" The older man responds. They sit together and have a drink. I can feel Jack's disgust in our counterpart and the feeling is mutual.

When leaving he gives the older man a hug anyway. The air starts to warp. The women in captivity start to yell and scream. The older gentleman, Jack, starts to expand. His skin stretches as he moans and yells loudly. Then he literally explodes.

Jack from Jack's shack is covered in the older man's blood and skin. Jack starts panicking and runs back to his transfer location. He slides back to Perfect Earth and rushes to a small creek behind his shack. He scrubs and scrubs the blood off until his skin starts to turn bright red.

He feels hatred and a wrath he has never known seep through his body. Then he hears a knock.

He opens the door. There is Elizabeth. She is yelling about fake medicine given to a girl in the neighborhood. He hears nothing. Then he grabs her. He wants to be in control.
He is.

I want to look away. I do not want to see him taking Elizabeth for himself. I try to look another direction. Wherever I look, the scene plays. The horror of his act never sets in.

He validates it.

He needed it.

He could not control it. After all he is just a man with needs.

After that he stays in his shack. He does not venture out. His contact with Sharon is the first in years. Next, I see him chained to the floor of the courthouse. He is blaming Ella. She stands up for him anyways. Then I see the gun.

It all goes black.

My head is fuzzy as I come to. Thinking I am waking up from a weird dream, I find I am no longer in my cell.

I am standing over a pile of dead bodies.

The stench almost knocks me back out.

Chapter 26

Bodies

~ *Ella* ~

Opening my eyes, I see a sliver of light.

The smell. My god, the smell almost knocks me back out. The smell of decaying flesh and the squishy harshness of it propped up on bones. I look to my right, and I see his face. Jack's face. I open my mouth to say, "oh thank god, you are here Jack," but the smell enters my mouth. I can taste the rottenness and I start to gag. The vileness creeps up my throat and I swallow it back down.

I touch Jack's blood-covered face and he does not move. His eyes are still open. Still on me, but he is gone. Then it all comes back. The court room, him being shot. I want to cry. I want Lindsey. *'Please, please, please Lindsey I cannot do this alone. I need you, please.'* I cry out in my head. She does not respond. She is not there.

So, I start to push through, towards the sliver of light. I feel something gooey moving on my arm. A grey maggot is making its way across to find its next home. I shudder a shudder that goes through my entire body, down to my toes. I push forward.

I poke my head out the bright light blinding me. Pulling myself up, out of the jelly-like prison. I hear it all squish. The body parts, the people, and again I swallow hard. Eventually, I am on top of the pile of dead bodies. I start to carefully climb down. Then I see her.

I freeze in my tracks.

"Ella." Elizabeth says. She opens her mouth to say more, then shuts it. She was the girl from my dream. This is my dream which Lindsey does not help me through. I had never gotten this far. *What happens after the pile of bodies?*

"Hey Elizabeth," I say, and it somehow comes out more casual than I expected, as if we just ran into each other in the street. This makes me laugh. I laugh a laugh that I haven't since I was with Amanda in the woods before my twelfth birthday. Everything has changed so much since then. Hell, everything has changed so much since yesterday. Tears start to spill out of my eyes as I laugh.

Elizabeth looks terrified.

I can imagine how I must look, covered in blood, on top of a pile of dead bodies, laughing and crying. My hair frizzed out and plastered to my head with sweat. It just makes me laugh more.

Finally, I start to calm down. My breaths are ragged and laced with hiccups as I slide down the side of the pile.

"You could have put me a little closer to the top ya know?" I say to Elizabeth.

"How do you know her? How do you know my true mother?" Elizabeth still looks terrified. I remember the words Lindsey told me to say. The words meant for Elizabeth.

"She is kind of a part of me, I guess. It is hard to explain. How do you know her? How is she your mother?" Elizabeth crumbles to the ground and through tears tells me about Lindsey. The bond they had. The things she learned from her. The brutal end. How little Elizabeth tried to run after her, but she was no match for a tiger. How she went to the pool behind the birthing facility. The one Lindsey had told her about and sat in it yearning for connection. How she has never been able to find her. The anger that she feels every day for Lindsey not taking her with her. The image of her tyrant of a mother's face being mauled in front of her. She tells me how she wondered back home hoping to cry in her father's arms but instead found him swinging from a rope in Lindsey's room. All of it.

All that Elizabeth has carried with her for the past 18 years.

Tears fill my eyes as I realize the significance of this moment. Elizabeth and I, side by side, raised and protected by the same tigress woman. The woman who had broken barriers. The woman who, without her, I would not have stood up for Jack. Elizabeth would have killed her baby. The woman who taught us that caring, and kindness are powerful and mean something. Even if we both fail at it too often. We sit in silence, holding each other sobbing. I wish Lindsey could tap in for this moment. I wish she could share it with us.

Then I remember her panic, I remember what she said about the pool. Lindsey needs me.

"Do you remember where that pool is, Elizabeth? I need to go home." I say glancing around. We are in the middle of the Jungle.

"Yes, I do. What does the pool have to do with you going home?" She asks.

"You will see. Trust me, if you are meant to, you will find your pool one day too." I smile. We get up and start the journey. A similar journey Lindsey would have run on all four paws eighteen years ago. Except this time, I know where the pool leads.

Or at least I think I do.

When we arrive, we hug each other for what seems for a long time. I want to take her with me. I do not want to leave her in this world of masks.

"You smell awful." Elizabeth says pulling back wiping her hands on her navy-blue dress in disgust.

"Well you know somebody shot me and threw me in a pile of dead bodies." I laugh and she smirks back. "What will you do now?" I ask, as we step back from our embrace.

"Protect my daughter and actually make some kind choices. Maybe I will run away with Henry and Lindy after all. Maybe I will find my pool and take them with me..........Thank you for bringing my mother back to me. I cannot repay you enough. What will you do?" She asks.

"I am not sure. I guess I will see what is waiting for me. Try your childhood hideout. The place from a time you connected with nature the most." I step into the pool of water. Elizabeth watches with her beautiful blue eyes welling with tears. I sit down and feel my own eyes prickle with tears. Then the earth starts sinking beneath me.

Black is all around me as once again I move through space. My stomach does flips, as if two angry mermaids are fighting inside my ocean of a belly. I grind my teeth together, thinking over and over that I will be reunited with Lindsey soon.

THUMP! I feel ground beneath me.

I sit up but everything blurs out as I turn over to finally vomit.

Chapter 27

Hunger

[Lindsey]

On Ella's fifth birthday, Bob and Wendy had the house crawling with children and parents. They had decided they were going to throw Ella a party. That many people around the house would put me at risk, so I almost changed their minds. However, little Ella was so excited that I couldn't bring myself to do it. So, I decided I would celebrate Ella growing, by hunting in the woods.

I was stealthily leading my second kill, a small brown rabbit, towards me, when I heard a crack. The birds chirping around me silenced. All the other animals and I could feel it. We had an intruder.

I slowly crept behind the tent of branches I had been making for Ella. That is when I saw a dark figure emerge from behind a tall oak tree about twenty paces away. He was wearing a suit, which I found comical for the woods. He had pale skin and his face was skinny and sunken. His hair was light brown. My favorite feature was not his lanky arms and legs, his erect way of walking, or his nervous tapping of his fingers on the side of his pant leg; it was his handlebar mustache.

As I was musing about his ridiculous appearance, I barely noticed the plump bearded man standing behind him. His face was patchy red and looked like it could explode at any moment. He spit a dark liquid out of his crammed teeth. He was also wearing clothes with leaves all over them. However, they were a shade too dark for the bright green summer haze that hung around the forest. The most alarming part of this man was his weapon. It was not like the dart or stun guns I was used to seeing. It had a long tube with a wooden handle.

It was so slender.

"Where'd she go? I told you she's a fast un'", the plump man said.

"Be quiet Timmy. I expected that as the pro hunter you claim to be, you would understand the importance of silence and patience." The handlebar mustache spat out the last two words in frustration. I was so surprised the plump man was a hunter. I could never imagine him ever being quick enough to catch an animal. The image almost made me giggle.

Now I know he most likely used his weapon.

"We are not here to hurt you. I just want to speak to you about your home. I know where you are from. Perfect Earth is something I, myself, have been studying for years. It has amazing history and the journey to optimal environmental and economic status is astounding. Please, I am only asking for information." The handlebar mustache guy said loudly. I tried to tap into his mind. He sounded so sincere, but it felt wrong. I tried until my nose bled. His mind was completely locked up. *Why would I not be able to tap into his mind? Is he from where I'm from?* I needed to know. However, the weapon and bearded man was a problem.

He was itching for a kill; I could feel it.

So, I tapped into the plump gentlemen's mind. *'Run. This man cannot be trusted. He is planning on feeding you to the woman of the wood. Take your weapon and run.'* On cue he turned around swiftly and ran out of the woods shouting and hollering. I knew it was not smart to have me planted in his mind at all, but I would worry about that later. Now it was time to talk to the handlebar mustache guy.

I moved quickly and quietly towards him. He was wringing his hands nervously. I came out from the oak tree behind him.

"How do you know where I am from?" I spoke. He turned around quickly and stared in complete awe. He opened his mouth, and a squeaking noise came out. I continued to stare into his eyes waiting for a response.

"Hello, my name is Steve. I am with a universal organization, the Agency. Our goal is to create the optimum society in this dimension. That is why I have studied Perfect Earth, your earth. We want more information about the government's role there and the people. We want to know how to reach such perfection." Steve stammered.

"My earth is not perfect in any way. It is beautiful, but that is about it. It was nice meeting you, but I have hunting to do." I replied. I started to turn around to go back into hiding.

"NO PLEASE! You do not understand. I know there are many enslaved people there, but that is a problem we can fix. You and me, together. We want to take all the perfect parts of your world and fix what needs fixed to create an optimum living space for all. Please. I need your help. By helping me, you could help others." I stopped.

"How? How could you possibly fix it?" I glared. This man had no idea what he was talking about.

I know that now.

"We have already created a safe space for Humbles on Perfect Earth. We are going to gradually bring Humbles into this space. We are going to improve both earths. We can all help each other. We already have a Humble, Susan, who has also found her way to us. She is helping groom the next slider. We just finished a mission with two Humbles, but it failed after they were both recognized. We need people from this world who are young, smart, and strong. People who are optimistic. People who can make a real change. We can't do it without you and Susan. You know your world better than we do. You understand it. Please, we need your help." Steve said.

"Why can't I read your mind?" I replied.

"For the same reason I can't read yours. Now I have a question for you. Why do you hunt in human form? I assume you are a predator?" Steve smiled.

"I haven't been able to change into my cat form since I arrived here." I reply.

. . . .

That is how I met Steve. A man who seemed to genuinely believe in his cause. A man who truly believed in me, or at least I thought he did.

Now what stands in front of me is a power-hungry piece of a human. He has gotten lost. The anger is building up in me as I calmly stand, chained up against the wall. I watch as he injects Susan's head with a large needle.

"Truly, Lindsey, thank you for your work. We got so much intel on this trip. My buddies in the organization tell me that little Miss Ella is being taken care of. Don't you worry.", Steve says.

We are in the In Between, in the same exam room where Ella was injected with her tracker. I want to tell her so badly to take it out. I used everything I had to reach Elizabeth, but I could not. You cannot tap into people from your world. That is something Steve taught me long ago. Because of this, my Ella is dead.

I feel numb all over.

How could I let this happen? I watch in a daze as Susan, strapped onto the table shakes violently. Foam exits her mouth, and her eye lids shudder up and down. This is the end. This is how Steve chose to end it. To put us down, like the animals we are. There never was a safe haven. There never was a 'we'. There was him and the Agency after money. They got the answers they need to put systems in place to hold people down. Systems that decide who wins and who loses. Systems that break people down. Systems that pit people against each other. Because only eight percent holding all the money and power is not so bad when you are at the top.

I watch as Susan's body comes to a halt. Steve is about to start talking when I feel it. My mind awakes.

I feel the water move and the feet step in. Ella is alive. She is using my portal to get home. I feel her pain and despair. She is in the tent I built for her. She is home safe. She is calling my name. I am overfilled with joy. She made it; she is alive. I feel her eyelids close and I tap into her dream one last time. I tell her I love her.

I show her our origin.

"LINDSEY!! LINDSEY!! Wake upppppp! I do not want you to miss this dear." Steve slaps me hard in the face.

Tears well up as I say goodbye to Ella and come back into the room.

"Have you heard a word I have said Lindsey? I want to give you the proper goodbye you deserve. You were always my favorite," Steve says, as my eyes set on his. "You know I have always thought it a shame that you cannot enter to your cat form. Watching Humbles revert to what they really are has always fascinated me." Steve's eyes twinkle as he taunts me.

Steve has never truly known anything. I realize he has never known what type of cat I am. He probably assumes I am a house cat. He has always underestimated us.

I let myself feel the pain and thirst I have suppressed this entire mission. The thirst for a hunt. The hunger for a fresh kill. Not the processed and cooked meat Steve has been serving me. Not the sliced veggies and rice. The warm metal taste of fresh blood. That is what I want. That is what I've been missing. I have gone through headaches and hunger for Ella. To concentrate. To keep her safe. She will be fine. She will go home and find that her loving parents missed her. She will either live a normal life or take my advice and let another part of herself become more whole. Either way, Ella will be fine.

So, I can indulge. I feed in.

Steve takes off my chains and zip ties my hands as he starts to lead me to the surgical table.

I feel myself changing into my tiger form. It is like putting a pair of sweatpants on after wearing jeans for twelve hours. It just fits.

I watch as Steve looks in horror.

"I thought you were a cat", he stammers. I snarl in his face. I let a loud roar escape my mouth. I watch his lips quiver and he starts ringing his hands nervously like the day we first met. I break the zip ties around my paws.

He tries to run, and I chase him.

I pace, blocking the exits whenever he tries to make a run for it. I pounce, giving him a scratch there and here. He lets out high pitched squeals with each mark I give him. I watch as he bleeds and continues to weaken. He crawls on his hands and knees, sobbing and begging me to stop. I forgot how fun it is to play with your food. His sobbing turns into screaming and wailing and the sounds hurt my ears.

It is time.

It is time to eat.

Chapter 28

Fall

~ Ella ~

The smell of sweet, damp minerals hit my nostrils as I sit up. I wait for the bright white light to take over my vision, but I am not in the In Between. My old friend, the forest, comes into view. Not the green leafy view I had left behind. Not the live branches that I was breaking with my large betrayers' feet.

It is fall.

Near the end of fall.

Many of the branches are bare and I am sitting on layers of wet, fallen red, orange, and brown leaves. The sky is overcast grey, as if the water falling from the sky just left but is not sure if she wants to stay or go. I am in my tent of branches. I am back home. This is not where I am supposed to be. I am supposed to be with Lindsey. She should be telling me how to get Jack back. I know he died. I know I saw his decomposing body, but that cannot be it. It just can't. Now I know there are three other earths, so *can't there be other Jacks? Would they be my Jack? Where is Lindsey?*

'Lindsey!! Please I need you. This is not where I wanted to come to. I need to find you. We need to bring back Jack. LINDSEY PLEASE!!!' I scream in my head so loud my temples ache.

The lump grows bigger in my throat. I angrily stand up and bang my head on one of the branches. This time I scream out loud. Louder than I have screamed in my entire life.

"LINDSEYYYY PLEASEEEEEE! I NEED YOU! YOU ARE THE ONE PERSON WHO CAN'T LEAVE!" Anger flows out of me as I kick the stick tent with all my might over and over. Tears are streaming down my face. I hear cracking. I don't know if it's me or the branches, but I don't care. I feel my body collapse onto the wet ground. This spot that has relieved me from my life so many times. Now it is just the ground. I pound, hoping it will open and swallow me back in.

"You are the one person, Lindsey." I murmur over and over. My body, my mind, and I are just plain exhausted. I have no idea what time, day, month, or year it is. I know I should walk to the little house on the hill, but my brain has a different plan.

I drift off to sleep, propped up on a pile of broken branches.

I feel her. I feel Lindsey. I know I am asleep, and I want to open my eyes. I want to get up and shout "you came back for me!". I can't. Like old times, my body will not move, and she has control of my mind.

I am walking into the old house on the hill. I turn back the long hallway and my feet make a loud noise on the hard wood floor with each step. I am heading towards the back room. My room. I open the door slowly and the strong smell of cigarettes hangs in the air. This is weird because I know mother does not smoke. She hates smoking. The smoke clears and my room is decorated how it was when I was a child. Peach walls and a peach frilly bed spread. My dolls are lined up on the bed. Then all three of them wink in unison. Then their eyes go to the chestnut hope chest at the foot of my bed. There are three dainty fingers with barbie pink nail polish poking out. My heart is pounding, and I want to run. Unfortunately, I am still not controlling my body.

I slowly lift the chest lid and I am welcomed with a creak. Inside is a beautiful slim woman with a perfect figure and she is wearing all pink. She looks so familiar. Her blue eyes are still wide open, but the light has completely left them. Maybe her eyes never had them. Then with panic I drop the lid and it crunches her fingers.

It is Ally. Ally, Elizabeth's mom, is the beautiful dead woman in my hope chest. The closet door creaks open, and I hear a women's unhinged laughter. Cigarette smoke rolls out as the door continues to open. The woman inside the closet has long stringy hair, brown eyes, and perfect white teeth. Her neck fat is swaying back and forth as she laughs. She stops, suddenly, and looks straight at me.

It is a fatter, more human version of Lindsey.

"She won't cross me again. Not ever again. That one has always been sneaky, using family as an excuse for everything," she spits out, and then rolls her head back and continues to laugh.

As she laughs, she takes a looped rope that is hanging from the ceiling of the closet and puts it around her neck. She stops to take another puff. Her laughing face drops to a normal gaze and I can see every crease and line. She looks about seventy years old. She opens the little door and pulls out James. I hold my breath thinking she is about to shoot herself.

Instead, she hands it to me.

"James is the answer, little one. It is what brought you and I together. He can bring us together again." She smiles a kind smile. A smile so genuine that I believe it truly is Lindsey. A smile that makes me forget Elizabeth's dead mother is stuffed into a hope chest behind me. She climbs up to stand on the chair she has been sitting on. She pulls the string hanging from the single light bulb that lights my small closet.

The room goes dark, and I hear it all.

The choking and gasping for air. The creaking swing of her body hanging from the ceiling. I close my eyes and open them again trying to make it all go away.

In the corner of the closet, I see glowing green eyes filled with tears. My Lindsey's eyes. But they are smaller and do not have the woman I know behind them. They have a child's innocence still stitched in.

I try to move forward to hug her, but I cannot move.

Chapter 29

Watch it Burn
JACK

I gasp and then start to immediately gag. The smell of the bodies is horrible. I start to vomit. I wipe my mouth and see vomit and blood on the back of my hand. I reach up and wince as I touch my still broken nose and gash on my forehead. *What have I done?* I wonder if Ella is okay. Then I feel someone's eyes on me. I turn around quickly and there she is.

Elizabeth.

"What the hell are you doing here?", I say. It comes out harsher than I intended. I can't get the scene of what was done to her out of my head. Looking at her makes me feel so much shame.

"It's time, Jack.", she says locking eyes with mine.

"Where's Ella?", I ask wiping my hands on my pants nervously.

"She is safe. I promise. Look, I am not the evil person you think I am. I just have to wear a lot of different hats to survive.", she is intently staring into my eyes. "I meant what I said. I like your idea. We need to burn it down before we rebuild it. I want to rebuild it for everyone. I just don't know how."

"So you are letting me burn it to the ground?", I ask with excitement welling up inside my chest. My time has come.

"How are we going to rebuild it?" She turns her gaze to the ground and wrings her hands. She expects me to have the answer to this. I do not know how to build a fair world. I have been so concentrated on destroying everything, that I have no idea how to build it back up. How do I tell her that? How do I admit that I have no plan? How do I admit I don't want to be part of one? How do I say out loud that I like chaos and never have thought about what happens when all is ash and I am the last man standing?

"I hadn't gotten that far yet." I stare at her exuding confidence.

"Well, the courthouse is all locked up. It's all yours Jack." She walks over to the edge of the trees and grabs a bottle of gasoline and a match. She sets them down in front of me. Then keeps walking without another word.

. . . .

When I arrive at the courthouse, I can hear them screaming inside. They want me to let them out. I slowly circle the building squirting gasoline on the walls. The glug glug glug of the liquid is soothing.

After I have circled the entire building, I light a match and drop it on the trail of gasoline leading to the door. It all catches fire. The screams. They are awful. The screams get louder and louder.

I just stand and watch.

Then something inside explodes and the roof of the building falls in. The front wall crumples. A woman on fire flees out screaming. The smell.

I want to vomit again.

I need to get out of here. I start to run. I run as fast as I can until I end up in front of Jack's shack.

I go to the door of the metal capsule. I do not know how to set up the machine coordinates. I just hit the green button assuming that means start and I step in. The machine groans louder and louder. Just before I start to sink. I hear someone calling my name in the shack. I am about to open the door when the ground sinks below me. I start to fall and fall. My vision is starting to go in and out.

I whisper a little lullaby in my head to sooth my mind.

"Still red. Flickering Red.

Accompanied by black smoke, all is well.

Pour fast. Scratch hard.

Look as walls become charred.

Sweat beads. Blue veins.

Watch as they squirm in pain."

– Jacks lullaby.

Chapter 30

James is the Answer
~Ella~

I sit up quickly, drenched in sweat and dampness. It is starting to get dark. I go to stand up and pain shoots up from my foot. I slowly take off my dirty shoe and see my middle toe is black and blue and swollen.

"A toe for a toe huh Jack?" I say out loud followed by a scoff at the irony. I painfully shove my shoe back on and start to hobble my way through the woods. My woods.

Being a stranger once again makes me grimace, but I need to get to the house on the hill. My hobbling journey takes about an hour, and it is completely dark when I arrive to the house.

All the lights in the house are off, which surprises me, as I would always leave at least one on. Maybe the light bulb went out. I walk to the front to grab my spare key from the fake rock, but everything is different. There is a beautiful brand-new white front porch with a porch swing. The porch swing has beautiful, embroidered pillows on it of birds. I think of Sharon. Jack's screechy protector. I wonder if she is with Lindsey.

My rock is not in its normal place, and I find it buried halfway beneath a bush. My key is still there. I slowly unlock the now bright blue door and enter my house on the hill.

It smells of gum drops and lavender not stale smoke and teenage body odor. I walk quietly to the kitchen. I am starving. Everything in the kitchen is bright blue and aquatic themed, as if I stumbled upon a beach house. This is not my house on the hill.

Regardless, there is a fridge, and my belly is rumbling. Everything in the fridge has the word organic on it. This almost makes me laugh. What a weird word to put on food. I grab some organic mozzarella cheese and organic tomatoes and take turns biting into one and then the other. Once I have made it through the entire fist size ball of cheese and one full tomato, I grab a newspaper laying on the counter. The headline reads "Today Marks the 5 Year Anniversary of the Disappearing Girl". I open it fully to see a picture of me grinning awkwardly.

It's my senior year picture; the one of me leaning against the tree. That seems so long ago. There is also a picture of my mother crying and dad with his arm around her, glaring at the camera. I gasp out loud. A little too loud. I hold my breath for a couple of minutes, waiting for whoever decided to make my kitchen aquatic to come out yelling. No one stirs. I do not even know if anyone is here.

Five years.

I went on a two-week mission and somehow it has been five years. That puts me at twenty-three years old. When people travel through space and time in movies and books, they always come back with no time passing. I guess that is not how it really works.

I bring my mind back to why I am here. I need to get James out of the closet. I need to figure out how a gun could be the answer to anything.

I slowly step towards the hallway. It has been freshly painted a white color, rather than the orange color that was stained with black streaks. I pause at my parent's bedroom door. Part of me wants to see if they are cuddled in their bed.

I refrain.

I continue to the back bedroom on the left. I half expect to open the door and see my old peach bedroom set, like in the dream. Instead of peach frills, it is white frills with a white canopy. There is a little girl curled up, surrounded by what looks like fifty stuffed animals. Her little eyebrows are furrowed together, as if she is dreaming of the most difficult math problem. I walk around my room slowly and quietly.

It is completely different.

Everything has changed.

I pick up a picture frame on her nightstand. The frame has pink roses with bright green vines on off white. It is hand painted. The picture is of her with a man and a woman. I squint because the man and the woman look exactly like my parents. I put it down and pick it up again. I want to make sure my eyes are adjusting appropriately. It still looks like them. Then I look around her room and they are in all her pictures. My parents. *Why on earth are they in all these pictures? Did I slide back to the wrong Earth?* I panic with the room swirling around me. I start to turn around to run when a Barbie hand lodges itself into my bad foot. Pain shoots up my leg. I let out a whimper involuntarily. The little girl starts to wake up.

I quickly slip into the closet.

"Mommyyyy!!" She shrills. She starts crying. I hear my mother's footsteps. I can tell they are hers by the bounce and lightness of them. I peer through the crack of the closet door. "Mommy, there is a woman in here. I swear, mommy, she's going to hurt me.", says the little girl.

My mother looks sad and distant for a moment.

"No honey, it's just a bad dream. You know, I once knew a special little girl just like yourself, and she also had bad dreams. You know what I would do when she had bad dreams?" My mother is almost crying.

"What mommy?" The sweet little girl answers.

"I would rub her back just like this and hum softly." She starts to hum. A tune I had blocked out of my mind. A hot tear slides down my cheek as I hear my childhood lullaby. She was there for me in the beginning. I remember the paper. The picture of her crying. Maybe she really did care for me this whole time. Maybe, with this little girl, she won't leave like she left me. Hopefully.

I know I can't stick around to find out. What would I even tell her? That I traveled to an alternate version of our earth, got someone killed, and failed at making any change? That I went on a two-week mission that turned into a month-long mission that changed me. That I am not even close to the resentful high school girl that left this place. That I left Lindsey somewhere out there and I don't how to reach her. But I do have an idea, I have James.

My mother stands up and she glances towards where I stand. She crosses the room and I hold my breath thinking she is about to open the door. Instead, she shuts it and I hear her footsteps pad down the hallway back to her room. I feel the wall of the closet in the dark for the little door and pop it open. James is still in his home. This gun gifted to me by my father. This gun I named after my mother's true love in an alternate dimension. This gun I named after my middle name that I use to hate.

James is the answer, the suicidal Lindsey had said. *How is James the answer? How do I get Jack and Lindsey back?* Then, in the dream, the green eyes glow from the corner of the closet. I catch myself glancing over my shoulder, expecting them to be there.

That's when it clicks.

You can only enter another dimension if you do not exist there. Your soul is connected to the four pieces of yourself; as one dies, you can enter another. Jack died in Perfect Earth, but there are two other Earths. Lindsey killed herself in this one, just as my Lindsey exited hers. Their paths crossed and that is how my Lindsey came here.

That is how our journey started.

The room is still, and I know it is time for me to find the answer. There is just one thing left to do. I make my way back to the kitchen and find the chef's knife I fell on what seems like so long ago. I stand over the sink and push the tip into my neck. It hurts as warm blood trickles down. I reach in and pull out the microchip and drop it in the trash can, knowing the trash will be carried away from the house on the hill. Holding my bleeding neck, I make my way back to the back bedroom. I look at the little girl one last time. I am still holding the knife and gun.

I creep over to the window and push it up slowly and climb out, careful to not make any noise. I fall out onto all fours and feel the damp soft grass between my fingers. I head up to the top of the field.

The night is cold and thick. I walk through the tall grass as it slivers around my legs. It is as if it knows and is making room for me. I drop the knife into the ground, as it starts to feel too heavy. Blood continues to trickle out of my neck and down my arm. It sprinkles onto the tall cattails that continue to part for me. Every step feels as if my feet have fifty-pound bags of sand on top of them. My lungs act as if I have just finished running a marathon.

The thickness surrounding me pulls me back to the house on the hill. The thought of the comfy couch that would hug my body and keep me warm and safe. The thought of my mother's and father's arms around mine. The joy they would get from knowing I am safe and home.

The little house on the hill, however, does not belong to me anymore. I am just another one of its ghosts. That house was full of loneliness, my childhood, and possible adventure. Now it is filled with someone else's dreams and nightmares. Anger fills up inside of me. Eighteen years. Eighteen years she watched over me and now she is just gone. She showed me another world. She showed me the reality of my dreams and what 'perfect' really means to people. She showed me what perfect should mean to me. She showed me who I am, and I somehow just came back here.

This is all I have left, this little house on the hill, and it is now filled with someone else's things. Even my parents are different. I changed them; I could see in their smiles in the picture. They have already lost one daughter and they are not going to lose this one. They will be there for her. They will soothe her nightmares. They take her with them on their fancy trips.

It is just me.

The person who sat there and condemned the love of her life. The person who yelled for her protector, knowing that she left her somewhere out there.

Yes, I might be insane.

Putting a gun to your head is a taboo way to solve your problems.

But I know things of the universe that others do not. I have seen the world in a completely different way. I know that pulling this trigger just might lead me to a different destiny. I also know that it might just end me, here, for I am not entirely sure where else I exist. *Do I really want to bring another version of myself here to this Earth?*

I pull the cold barrel to my temple. I am not scared, because a part of me died when I left Fernweh and this might lead me to where my true loves are. Just maybe. Jack, Lindsey this is all for you. This story, this sacrifice.

One breath in and a swift pull of the trigger is all I need to do.

One breath.

My finger on the cold metal.

Suddenly my eyes roll back, and I feel white light shoot through my body. Looks like I will not be bringing any part of me back here. She is calling on me first.

We're coming for you, Jack and Lindsey.

We will be reunited soon.

References

Italian Shoe Factory. "How Shoes Are Made: Step by Step." *Italian Shoe Factory*,
    15 May 2019, https://italianshoefactory.com/blog/how-shoes-are-made/.

Polygyan. "Visualize the 4th, 5th & 6th Dimensions." *Medium*, Medium, 14 Jan.
    2021, https://polygyan.medium.com/visualizing-higher-dimensions-i-
    5dbbfbc8ac2f.

Hawking, Stephen. *The Theory of Everything: The Origin and Fate of the
    Universe*. Jaico Publishing House, 2009.

www.ingramcontent.com/pod-product-compliance
Lightning Source LLC
Chambersburg PA
CBHW071511170626
46811CB00007B/2818